TIME & TEMPER

TIME & TEMPER

BEASTS OF LONDON

NATANIA BARRON

Charlotte, NC

FALSTAFF
BOOKS

WWW.FALSTAFFBOOKS.COM

For Olga, who gave me the world.

LANDLEGS

We begin again. This time, not with the lamia known as Nerissa Waldemar, nor with the unicorn known as Christabel Crane, but with a sylph who calls herself Vivienne du Lac. You will recall her adventures came to a rather abrupt halt some twenty years ago when she was taken, quite unfairly in her opinion, and sold in bondage. The previous volume, *Masks & Malevolence*, features her sparingly on account of her life falling into the sad, monotonous patterns of servitude she would prefer left untold.

But now, things begin to change. And with change, sometimes, comes hope. At least, we sincerely wish that is the case for Vivienne. She has been out of the picture a bit too long, and nothing perturbs her more than being overlooked.

So, Vivienne finds herself in Spain, of all places, and in Andalusia more specifically. She has arrived by boat and is quite vexed at the state of the villa once they reach it. She has no right to be—unlike in years past, she has no claim to the arrangement—but this is still considerably worse than her master's usual fare. Even with her magical capabilities sincerely dampened, she has not lost her knack for seeing details and quality. Though her master is many things, he is not typically one to skimp on luxury. So, she deduces that something must be amiss.

A few years ago, that fact might have kindled a bright glimmer of hope in her, finding a weakness in her bondage, but now she feels only a low, distant memory of optimism. How strange it is to grow accustomed to enslavement after so many centuries of freedom. Millennia, even. She has rather lost track. And though she has only been in bondage for twenty years, Vivienne feels the weight of that time more than any other in recent memory. Though if she digs deep enough…

As if in acknowledgement of her mere thoughts, the thin bangles on her wrists pulse with a hot current of magic, a searing counterpoint to hope. There is no doubt now. Her master is near.

Vivienne has been waiting, sitting on a large, moth-eaten suitcase, in the central garden of the villa. She knows the routine by now. She is to wait for her master. And even though her arcane power surges beneath her shackles, she is helpless to do anything other than wait. And Vivienne du Lac has never liked waiting. Not that it matters any longer.

The servants scurry as the master's footfalls echo across the terracotta tiles, boot heels reverberating with every step, crunching against the detritus of so many years upon the floor. Leaves skitter away from his presence as if they, too, were aware of his general poisonousness.

When Vivienne sees him, she feels the uncanny pulse of her shackles again, incapable of suppressing the sense of awe whenever in his presence. Which she resents. Woe to her for being such a helpless aesthete.

She likes to think there was an air of regret in Barqan's demeanor when he sold her to her new master. But she can only recall the djinni's final words to her: "Behold, a terror you do not know. May you drink deeply from that dark well, as I did."

She was busy at the time, rather preoccupied with the strange new circumstance of being bound in djinn-forged iron, and never asked the right questions. She honestly thought she would be able to escape.

Whatever happened to the djinni after that point, she does not know. It has been almost twenty years since her capture, and Barqan's affairs took him elsewhere. If not for the ultimate betrayal, she might almost miss him. If not for his droll company, or his treacle, which, when he was living as her servant, was second to none.

In the dim evening light—a strange, lingering light this close to the equator—her master's face is shadowed a moment under the balustrades and tree limbs stretching out overhead. Vivienne can tell he is wearing his good riding suit by the cut of his narrow shoulders. Maybe the navy one today. Or the tweed. She can make complaints about a thousand difficulties of being a thrall, but she must admit his taste in fashion rivals hers.

Nadine, the master's ifrit, greets him first, fussing over him and taking his coat and scarf. The ever-present blue light around her head illuminates his face just long enough for Vivienne to catch her breath. Like Vivienne, Nadine wears a chain; for her, though, the iron is about her neck.

Ah, yes, and there he is—her master. A chiseled face shaved clean as marble. There is not much mammalian about him other than the color and composition of his skin in its current glamor. He wears dark, round glasses to obscure his yellow eyes, but she rarely pays attention to them, anyway. It's his lips she likes, prone to smile and dip down in line with the widow's peak atop his head. A perfect V. A flawless specimen.

It's only when he talks that Vivienne notices the sharp teeth, the forked tongue, and she remembers what he is. She did live with a snake for centuries, after all, though not one full of such venom.

Her master, a man who goes only by a single name, is no lamia. Bastille, Lord of the Grey Moor, is a basilisk.

THE CELESTIAL TENANT

No snake has ever loved London so much as Nerissa Waldemar, of that she is confident. After far too long in the realms of sand and sun, she is now happily ensconced in a basement apartment in Shoreditch, reveling in the constant wet of the world, the chill tendrils of cool currents moving through the city, and the ever-present whisper of the Thames. Though she is a snake, she is a lamia, and as such prefers the wet to the dry, more like a salamander. She's never taken the time to ask why she is different from her other reptilian cousins; knowing certainly would not make life any easier, so she declines the research, even though Christabel would likely have hordes of research, and theories, on the subject.

In the three years since arriving in London, she has managed quite the setup for herself. She has a residence, for one thing, which she has taken the time to decorate to her tastes. Her tastes, such as they are, might be considered "bog chic" if there were such a thing, as she tends toward verdant hues and draping netting as decor, to better mirror the landscape of her nascent years. Granted, there was a great deal more bloodshed during that time, but she comforts herself knowing that, for the last seven years, she hasn't had to drink a drop of blood.

Her food source comes courtesy of the vampire network, an ancient and revered group of creatures living on the fringes of society. Though she does not claim kinship to them, two of them in Cairo, Beti and Micheaux, took her under their wing and provided a new way to feed: imp sweat. It is a silvery sweet stuff, a bit more expensive than she would like, but she only requires a small amount to keep her moving. Gone are the days when she had to fight tooth and nail to keep herself sated, breeding animals and pushing down her bestial needs to rend arteries and suck at bleeding flesh.

She doesn't even miss it. No, Nerissa is fully cured of her bloodthirst. If she finds herself panicking a little now and then if she doesn't get enough implet, as she calls it — a play on "gimlet"—she doesn't worry. This life is a better life. She is clearer of mind. She is sounder of body. She has time to decorate.

All but one corner of the apartment, that is. Behind a wooden screen, her companion Kit takes up residence, usually perched or dangling from the shelf she's installed for such use. Kit is a *kitsune*, a kind of fox spirit, who began her days as an unintentional slave, but now considers herself an official part of Nerissa's work chasing down monsters gone mad. Once, it was Goodwin and Waldemar. Then it was Goodwin, Waldemar, and Crane. Then things got complicated when Goodwin became an angel, which he'd always been, apparently, and Crane decided she needed an extended vacation. Now it's Waldemar and Kamiyama. And they make a very, very good team. Even if the name doesn't have quite the ring to it that she'd like.

So, it's been up to Nerissa and Kit to keep London safe

from Exigents and Aberrants, the monsters who either are driven to madness or else embrace it, for the last few years. In between her work, Nerissa has done all in her power to track down the kidnapper of her once (very unrequited) love, the sylph Vivienne du Lac. It has been twenty years since Vivienne, the one person who gave Nerissa a chance after she'd nearly gone Aberrant herself, was abducted, and they have little go to on concerning her whereabouts. They know a few things: her magic is most certainly dampened, because no one—not even the most sophisticated seers or birch benders—can locate her specific arcane imprint, which Christabel long ago derived during a holiday in Budapest.

Sometimes, Nerissa pretends that Vivienne is dead, because honestly to know she has quit the world and is at peace is better than thinking she is still in thrall to some genuinely abhorrent creature. But Nerissa, while scorned from a romantic sense, is sure that if Vivienne were to die, she would know. Their bond, while not of love in the sapphic sense, exists on another level of consciousness. The old snake may not be particularly religious—even among her closest friends, no particular pantheon makes sense, and so she relegates them all to the "geographical and cultural arcane"—but she does believe in the bond between people who share common experiences.

Which is also why she cannot ever quite do away with Christabel Crane or the angel. Or the dwarf. At this point, they have endured mad monsters hell-bent on destroying all other beasts, Egyptian goddesses with blood feuds, and the very tragic love story of a cherub who never seemed to get things quite right. And in between all that, dozens of arrests, imprisonments, and, thankfully, rehabilitations to her credit.

To some, Nerissa supposes, she is considered a traitor to her kind. But she genuinely appreciates humanity for what it is, which she has Vivienne to thank for, and does not think that they deserve to be considered food on a daily basis. They are, except for precious few, incapable of magic. Though their technology is disturbingly improving with every century, they are mostly powerless when it comes to defending themselves against the supernatural and arcane. Humans have a few redeeming qualities, she supposes. And also domesticated cats. She quite likes cats.

Life would be good—and it is, in moments—if Nerissa didn't consider herself a complete and utter failure. Despite her success in London, her friendship with Kit, and the fact she no longer must hunt for her food, she has nothing to show for the last twenty years of her life. Every year lived without Vivienne du Lac. What Vivienne would say about the décor of her Shoreditch apartment, she can only imagine.

And it isn't just Vivienne's absence, that constant gnawing shame of failure. Now, Nerissa must also check in on the angel every night, especially around the full moon when he is at his most melancholic and dramatic. That has gotten rather tiring as of late. He is so dull when he's in his divine form.

She misses Worth Goodwin, the insufferable newspaper-reading foppish monster the angel was before he was freed, even if he was a lie. And she knows Christabel misses him more. To say nothing of Vivienne, if she ever finds out.

Nerissa is just finishing her afternoon nap when someone raps on the door with light knuckles. A lovely side-effect of the implet is enhanced hearing. She discerns the precise hollow sound of more fragile fingers versus the hard pulse of meatier ones. As such, she knows it is Micheaux before the door is even opened. That, and the vampire wears so much cologne he's practically able to generate a personal miasma. The odor of *Quelleque Fleures* knows no limits when it comes to Micheaux.

As she opens the door, Nerissa takes in the garish figure of the French vampire. No matter how many times she sees him there's no less shock. He wears his hair in blond ringlets, tied with a different colored satin ribbon every day. Today it is shades of periwinkle blue that match his silk kimono and weskit below, emphasizing the bluish tone to his undead skin. But for the splash of blush at his cheeks and the gentle wrinkle of his forehead he would be otherwise indistinguishable from a corpse; a handsome, overwhelmingly floral corpse, but a corpse, nonetheless.

"My dear Ms. Waldemar!" Micheaux opens his arms wide in expectation of an embrace, or one of his cloyingly sweet kisses to the cheek, but Nerissa has learned how to evade him. "Micheaux has so very much missed you."

The lamia steps out of Micheaux's way and gestures inside the room. "Come, Micheaux. You are welcome."

Micheaux is delivering Nerissa's weekly store of implet, which he does not have to do and yet finds every reason to do so. Nerissa would wonder at his motives except she long ago realized the vampire was simply dim. If the fact that he always refers to himself in the third person isn't enough of a giveaway, his fashion sense would undoubtedly raise enough red flags. Silk, in October?

The phials in Micheaux's briefcase clink together and Nerissa feels a welling of anticipation rise in her. Food, glorious food. Nourishment. Not just sustenance. It is truly one of the most marvelous days of the week when the delivery comes, even if she must endure Micheaux.

Kit, who has been sleeping off her last adventure, stirs in her corner and Nerissa vaguely wonders if she's going to make herself known. Her dislike of the vampires is one of the most intense reactions Nerissa has ever seen, though Kit does seem to tolerate Micheaux when necessary.

"I hope you are enjoying the season," Nerissa says when Micheaux takes a seat on one of the less moth-eaten divans.

The vampire stretches out his long legs, looking down at

them as if for the first time, tilting his head to the side and gazing quizzically. Nerissa is just about to ask him if he's quite alright when he holds up a finger.

"Oh, Micheaux had a note to deliver, along with the food. Which is why Micheaux spent his time coming to this… unusual corner of London. It is so…quaint," he says with a smile in his voice. "Micheaux sees the angel is not around. That is good. Good."

The angel, Ophaniel, once Worth Goodwin, lives on the highest apartment in the building, sleeping most of the time and complaining away the rest.

"Ophaniel will likely require my attention later this evening," Nerissa says, doublechecking her watch. It conveniently displays the phases of the moon. A few years ago, she would have shunned such a piece of technology, but being the guardian of an angel means she has to work within her limitations. "But you still have time."

"He has the strangest eyes," Micheaux says, encircling his own with long, bony fingers. "Micheaux gets the feeling the angel is looking through him when he comes into view. Like a window and not a being."

"You likely don't have a soul," says Nerissa. "It's probably confusing for him."

"Micheaux likes to think he is enticing to the angel. But that is probably hoping for too much."

"Yes. The utter absurdity of such a match is beyond even my ability to imagine," Nerissa replies, glancing—but not meaning to—at Kit as she stretches and stirs a little more, pulling back the long, black curtain of her hair to reveal her eyes. Such behavior—sleeping upside down—used to bother Nerissa to no end. Now, she finds she quite appreciates the *kitsune*'s eccentricities. "Would you like some tea?"

Micheaux shakes his golden head, and Nerissa notes for the

first time that the vampire is wearing a wig. She hadn't realized that. Curious. And the veins on his face stand out a little starker than they used to. He doesn't look particularly well. It is difficult to measure illness in one who is already undead.

"Are you alright, Micheaux?" Nerissa tries not to adjust her glasses too obviously.

Micheaux smiles a wan smile. "Ah, well, there has been a good deal of drama within the coven. But when is there not? Micheaux does not like to get involved but finding rest has not been easy with all the yelling."

"I'm sorry," she says softly. "I know how essential sleep is for you."

"Perhaps one of these visits Micheaux will sleep right here for a few hours?"

"Yes, yes. Of course. But not today."

"Of course," whispers Micheaux. "But there is not much time today. Micheaux is due back soon." He starts staring at his legs again.

"The letter?" asks Nerissa.

"Oh, yes, yes. You really ought to read the letter. It's quite important, I think," Micheaux says.

Kit's voice drifts over from her corner. "You better not have read it, scoundrel." Scoundrel is one of Kit's favorite new words. For all her complaints about the English language, which she relates to the sound dogs make when they're chewing tough meat, she is always finding a new word or turn of phrase to master.

"Ah, fox woman," Micheaux says, all the delight of a child in his eyes. "Micheaux had hoped you might be here. Come into the light so Micheaux can see you."

"That would require me having to look at you, and such an arrangement would make my stomach turn," Kit says from the corner.

"Now, this letter," Nerissa presses before Micheaux can process the insult.

Micheaux makes a grand show of opening the long blue kimono and withdrawing a blood-red envelope from the interior pocket of his weskit. With every movement comes the unmistakable scent of *Quelleque Fleures,* along with that lingering, sickly sweet stench of death that all vampires emit. Like lilies at a funeral.

Nerissa takes the letter in her hand, curiously cold, and breaks the seal. It is from Beti, Micheaux's coven queen. She is a rather unassuming woman for a vampire, uncomplicated and homely for her sort, preferring the arts of herbalism and potions-making to hunting and devouring as most vampires do, which is a refreshing change. Now living in Paris, Beti is the eyes and ears of the underground monster community faction known as the Vampire Network, a growing group of supernatural beings who wish no harm to humankind, or so they claim. Nerissa and Kit have a tenuous alliance with them, if only because they supply enough implet for the lamia to keep healthy and hale.

Beti's handwriting is archaic and beautiful, spidery and flowery at the same time. She writes letters as surely as if they were letter pressed, and at first Nerissa is so enchanted by the script that she doesn't quite grasp the contents of the letter. So, she must read it again.

Dear Miss Waldemar,

It has been some time since our paths crossed, but I believe I have located your missing friend, or at least I know of her last whereabouts and the ship she came in on. It is now docked in the Thames, and I will be making a special trip to examine the stores there. Let us meet and then go onward to Spain, where Vivienne resided the last time I heard.

You are welcome to bring Mr. Goodwin/Ophaniel. But I would not suggest bringing the kitsune. And if Miss Crane is anywhere to be found, she may find it of some use as well.

    Most sincerely,

    Beti

Nerissa feels her jaw jump before she realizes just how hard she is biting down on her teeth. She can't say what feeling arises in her, but it is hope mingled with a strange kind of jealousy. How did the vampires come by such information? And so suddenly?

"This is remarkable," says Nerissa, turning the letter over in her hands as if in the hope that it might be a joke, or contain some note of clarification. But there is nothing. "Beti sent this to you?"

Micheaux looks taken aback. "Of course, she sent it to Micheaux. How else would Micheaux find it? We saw her ship a few hours ago, on our way here at twilight, and a little runner vampire brought this to Micheaux's attention."

Not for the first time, Nerissa wishes Christabel were here. It is abundantly clear that the situation is off. Micheaux looks sick, even for a vampire. The letter does not read in Beti's voice at all.

And the information is too good to be true.

"I apologize, Micheaux," the lamia says at last, folding up the letter. "It's only that we've been searching so long and so hard, with so many instances where we thought we had turned the final corner to see Vivienne that...well, I don't know what to say."

Kit takes the note, appearing in a swirl of color. She reads so fast that Nerissa startles when she says, "Well, I believe the proper phrase, in this case, would be 'thank you.'"

3

OF SELKIES AND SULKING

When you do not age or grow old, ten years can feel like the space of a few days. But when you're still mourning the loss of your would-be lover who turned out to be an angel and isn't exactly dead, but also isn't exactly alive, each day can feel like an eternity.

Such is the case for Christabel Crane. She has tried to bury herself in work, primarily research pertaining to creature spells, traveling through Ireland and Greece and India with Dr. Morgan Frye. Together they have proven a most impressive duo, doing more than twice the work Dr. Frye had managed in her many centuries alone.

While not an immortal per se, as Christabel is by way of being a unicorn, Dr. Frye is an unclassifiable being. She is as old as the earth. From her conversations, Christabel has deduced that the woman has always been present on the planet in one way or another, but most usually in her present state. Born and reborn, she retains all the memories of the time before her and collects that experience into a wickedly sharp mind and curious presence.

Christabel supposes that one might call Dr. Frye a

goddess. But the eccentric woman probably wouldn't like that. She's not one for formal titles or formalities of any sort, really. Dr. Frye is the kind of woman who wore trousers decades before they were fashionable. She refused corsets even in the height of the wasp waist, so when the twenties came roaring in, she was already ahead of the curve. Her hair is never to fashion, her language always a bit archaic, yet she never sounds out of date. And Dr. Frye is, always and forever, completely resistant to critique or general concern. Dr. Frye navigates the world with utter confidence and no need for affirmation. For Christabel's purposes, she has decided to think of Dr. Frye as a dragon.

They sit now among the rocks of the Outer Hebrides speaking to a young selkie named Jenn. Jenn's entire name is much longer, of a proto-Celtic derivation, and Christabel, to her surprise, rather likes the selkie. Christabel has never much cared for the sea nor the creatures in it. But as a selkie, currently in a seal state, Jenn is lovely. Her pelt is smooth as a pebble, reflecting the shining winter sun, silver and dark grey. Her eyes are like pools of dark water. And her voice is soft, lulling.

"Of course, when it comes to the frequency of selkie calls, well, it's entirely different than native speakers," Jenn is saying. Not only is she chief among her selkie sisters, but she is also an accomplished singer.

Christabel is trying to pay attention, but the moon is rising full over the bay of their little island, and she is thinking about Worth Goodwin again. Or, rather, Ophaniel, the angel he always was.

Dr. Frye leans forward, absorbing every word the selkie has to say. According to the doctor, such company is considered a great boon indeed, as selkies rarely share their secrets, let alone with strangers not from their islands. The only reason Jenn would speak to them at all was because Worth had contacted them a decade ago and had gained their trust by helping drain and dredge part of the bay so the selkies might better approach the island free from predators. Always generous, Worth Goodwin, even when he was supposed to be searching for Aberrants and Exigents with Nerissa and Vivienne.

"Fascinating," Dr. Frye says. "So, it is not simply a matter of wavelengths, as I had thought before." She is furiously scratching in her book, fingers ink-stained, eyes bright. How someone could be so old and yet still so in awe of the world is quite beyond Christabel. She's already beginning to tire of it, and she's scarcely forty.

"Yes, our throats are different," says Jenn, raising her head slightly to display the speckled area there. Hers looks like a little map. "Every selkie has a neck brand, as we call them. We name them, rather than ourselves. So, among my sisters I am called 'heather flower'—you see how my brand looks like a sprig of fresh heather?"

Christabel notes it looks almost like a sprig of heather. Or a side of bacon. Or a newt phallus. But she keeps those opinions safely to herself. As mentioned previously, she rather likes Jenn. And unlike her sometimes companion Nerissa Waldemar, Christabel can keep her thoughts inside her head.

"Our throats must be different," says Jenn, "for the change to occur. We are born of seals but possess the magic of women, so parts of each must be present in the other. But not entirely."

"Then your ears much be capable of receiving unique wavelengths as well," Dr. Frye continues.

"Oh, yes. We can even hear the stars," Jenn says with a glimmer in her dark brown eyes. "Though I have noticed that the swan constellation is a bit quiet as of late. We've been listening to her now and again…"

On a regular day, this would be fascinating for Christabel,

but she simply cannot abide by it any longer. She starts to stand and finds the selkie has sidled up next to her, looking up with sorrow in her eyes.

"It's the moon that concerns me," says Christabel. "It always makes me think of him."

Dr. Frye stops her furious writing and glances over her glasses at Christabel. "I've told you a thousand times, you don't have to be here with me. I can do the research on my own; though I can't argue that your help has been immense. Still, if I'm keeping you from him…"

"No, no, of course not, Dr. Frye," Christabel says. "I was lost in a moment of melancholy. It's been ten years, now. A quarter of my own, short, strange life. You would think I would have learned by now to accept that Worth Goodwin was nothing more than the phantasm—a costume—worn by Ophaniel to protect him."

Dr. Frye had a hand in the whole transfiguration of Ophaniel, and she so obviously feels guilty about it. "I was keeping him safe. I didn't think the persona would take so heartily. It is all a most unfortunate situation. How could I have anticipated a unicorn would fall in love with him?"

"I only thought I knew who he was—what he was," Christabel says.

"I didn't know what Worth was either if that's a consolation," Jenn says softly. "It wasn't easy to determine. Perhaps Dr. Frye's work was too good."

"You flatter me," says Dr. Frye. "It was old, strong magic. And I do wish the old fellow would stop being angry at me. Ah, well. I suppose I will incur Ophaniel's wrath to know he is alive, and that I kept him alive, despite the fury of a half dozen Egyptian deities."

Dr. Frye gives Christabel a sad smile.

"He's lucky to have you," says Christabel. "He just hasn't figured it out yet."

"There are a great many things Ophaniel hasn't figured out yet," says Dr. Frye with a snort. "I am very low on that list. Eventually, I hope, he will stop sulking and leave that tenement in Shoreditch, and we can have a proper discussion. But as it is, I have all the time in the world. And so does he. So, if it takes another ten centuries, so be it. I have waited before, and I will wait again."

Christabel wants to tell Dr. Frye that she feels the same way, that she will wait for Ophaniel. That she will hold out hope that Worth is there, somewhere. But she cannot. So, she falls silent and asks Jenn to sing a few more bars before the moon fully rises.

* * *

Over dinner that night in the cottage, Dr. Frye is frank with Christabel in a manner she has never been before. At first, Christabel is unsure what to do with such directness, but it doesn't take her long to feel a kind of relief in speaking freely about Worth. And Ophaniel.

"I cannot help but think this transformation is more difficult on you because of your very nature. Unicorns and angels falling in love…I would never have considered the ramifications in a thousand years." Dr. Frye never eats anything other than meat and mushrooms, with a sprinkling of vegetation now and then. Christabel prefers fruit and grains and always has to avert her eyes from the other woman's plate. Tonight, it is puffin breasts served rare, and it turns Christabel's stomach.

"It isn't angel and unicorns in love," Christabel corrects Dr. Frye. "We were not in love. We were not lovers."

"Ah, but your souls are connected."

"Even if that was the truth, Worth isn't *Worth*. He is gone."

Dr. Frye gives Christabel a pitying look that speaks

volumes. "I have told you this a few times before and I will tell you again, my dear. Nothing of Worth exists without Ophaniel. Worth was a refraction, a distillation of a facet of Ophaniel. You cannot make or destroy matter. I could not shape Worth from nothing."

"Ophaniel is nothing like Worth. He is a stuck up, narcissistic, self-centered prig."

"Well, you didn't give him much of a chance."

Christabel tries to argue, but it's true. When Ophaniel looked upon her and didn't know her, the fury and sorrow were so great she fled. For months, while Nerissa and Kit kept guard, Christabel traveled, only returning to London when absolutely necessary, sending money to support, and occasionally research on celestials, but remaining almost entirely out of the picture. Even now they are in London, not far considering Christabel's far-ranging adventures, arranging their lives to best fit around Ophaniel's, and she has no plans on meeting with them, in spite of Nerissa's pleading letters. The guilt rises and Christabel washes down the berry compote from her toast with a sip of weak wine.

"I didn't know what to do, Dr. Frye. Twenty years ago, I thought I was a clever young woman uncovering the truth about the supernatural. I had a purpose. I had a calling. I was headstrong and likely full of myself, but I was confident in many things. Worth was the one that made me question my place in the world, but to also seek my own truth. But then he also was the biggest threat to what I am," Christabel says in a rush of words and air. "He made me want *more* knowledge. He made me want…many things."

Dr. Frye chuckles into her glass of wine. Stronger. Redder. Older. The same words could apply to the doctor in contrast to the unicorn. "I do not think that making love will destroy you, if that's what worries you. An immortal life without a good bedding now and again is a sobering thought."

Saying it out loud makes Christabel cringe. "Everything I've read speaks to the purity of unicorns as a source of power. Of magic. What if it meant I would die?"

"Sex is very nice," Dr. Frye says matter-of-factly. "I'd say some would be willing to take that risk."

While Christabel gapes, Dr. Frye continues. "All I'm saying is that there's a striking lack of information about you and your kind. And while I do believe some of it has to do with the sheer rarity of unicorns as a whole, that doesn't stop me from suspecting there may be other forces at play. You may hold on to your purity and insist that you have no future with Ophaniel, or anyone else for that matter, but it is rather myopic, don't you think? The world is changing. What makes you think that we monsters don't change along with it? There is no point in making yourself miserable without the facts. We are close to having more information; I can feel it."

"But you have spent your whole life searching for evidence on the rarest of creatures. What makes you think that it will be different now?"

Dr. Frye gives Christabel a kind smile. "Because I found a unicorn after all, didn't I? It only took a few thousand years, but here you are. And if there's anyone who knows more about unicorns in the whole world, it's you. Though, to be honest, I hadn't expected you would have a fully human form. But that probably explains why unicorns are so difficult to track in the first place. You had to come from somewhere. Unicorns don't just appear fully fleshed from the earth. Even the worst among monsters have mothers."

"I was adopted," Christabel says. "I found that out during the trials."

Ah, yes, that was Christabel's other work. The Prague Agreements. She took two years in the late 20s to work side-by-side with two factions within the community of the arcane: gods and monsters. It is a long story and one deserving of an extended telling, but the short of it is that she worked to broker an alliance between the two sides. She helped determine, in a court of law no less, that monsters and deities are truly no different from one another. In fact, many stem from the same source entirely. Plenty of monsters are children of deities—and indeed, some gods are the progeny of monsters. This alliance has been somewhat tenuous but gained her renown. It also brought to light the confirmation of her adoption.

"Regardless, even orphans don't metamorphose from thin air," Dr. Frye says. "You can argue all you want, dear, but you are both woman and monster. You are a rare instance—and that, I'm quite certain, is how you won over the factions in Prague."

"I rather prefer the monsters," Christabel says quietly.

"I won't tell Hermes you said that."

Yes, that. Well. Christabel is trying to think of a clever retort when there comes a knock on the front door of the little cottage, and she is delighted. She did have something of a dalliance with Hermes, the Greek messenger god. He was charming and mysterious, and they had a lot to say…and do. But ultimately the god had no interest in being steadfast or exclusive, to say nothing of tiring of Christabel's hesitance in terms of romantic relations.

Still, she does miss him.

The women exchange looks at the sound of the door, and Dr. Frye immediately goes for her longsword, which never seems far from her hands. Christabel stands slowly, taking deep breaths. She knows that keeping calm increases her ability to fight tenfold. Though it's been ages since she's managed to transmute into her unicorn form, she must be prepared.

When Dr. Frye opens the door, however, it's just a delivery man. He is very young and wears a wispy red mustache with great pride. He looks terrified at the sight of Dr. Frye, as most men are. She towers above him, muscle and curves and smooth, sun-kissed skin. Her hair tumbles in dark waves, and her eyes pierce as sharply as her sword.

"Good evening," Dr. Frye says to the delivery boy.

He is practically shaking in his boots, but hands over the letter, anyway. He does not ask for a tip, and Dr. Frye unceremoniously shuts the door and looks calmly at Christabel.

"It's for you," she says. "It's from Nerissa."

Christabel takes the letter, immediately curious. Nerissa has done very little in terms of reaching out since the whole business with Worth and the Egyptian underworld; the lamia is not known for her transparency, and no matter how much they'd worked together in the past, Christabel senses Nerissa doesn't like her much. They have kept a courteous correspondence over the last few years, sharing notes and providing any useful clues about Vivienne du Lac. But Christabel now thinks is an unsolvable case, too difficult to crack, now almost twenty years after the sylph's abduction. The trail has run cold. Du Lac must be dead, or worse…

But the letter would not have her believe so.

"It says they know where Vivienne is," Christabel says. Dr. Frye does not know the entire business, but enough to be surprised.

"I'll be," Dr. Frye replies. "I had begun to think this sylph of yours was a collective hallucination. It's not unheard of…"

Christabel rereads the letter, looking for any code or sign it might be in jest. Even though she's quite aware of Nerissa's general lack of humor in any capacity, Christabel still finds it difficult to believe there is any kind of validity to the missive.

But it is written in Nerissa's same steady hand.

We do not know yet of the exact location, but we know it is in

Spain. Not far from Gibraltar. One of the servants at the facility somehow got word to the Vampire Network, and here we are.

The Vampire Network. Christabel has never liked them and wishes that it had been anyone but them involved. But then, she supposes it stands to reason that they would know. It's their business to know everything. Their currency is information.

"I suppose it's difficult for anyone to stay hidden for twenty years," Christabel says. "Even Vivienne du Lac."

"What a strange name," Dr. Frye muses. "It can't possibly be her real name. I knew the *real* Vivienne du Lac, and she was by no means a frivolous nymph."

"She's a sylph," corrects Christabel.

"Is she?"

"Yes," Christabel says. "And while she is vain and a bit conceited, she still does not deserve what has happened to her. All we know is that she is in pain, in trouble, and likely has been suffering for some time."

Dr. Frye raises an arched brow, pursing her lips. She looks almost childlike when she does that, the dimples in her cheeks deepening. "And you think it's likely that after two decades her captors simply decided it's not worth the effort to keep her concealed?"

"When you say it like that, no."

"I'm just saying that you should proceed with caution."

"I understand. And I'm sorry. It's just that we've been at this so long, and to have it conclude so abruptly. My intuition tells me that this is not as good as it appears. That there is something else at work here. But I worry for Nerissa."

"To say nothing of our angel."

Christabel hates it when Dr. Frye refers to Ophaniel that way. Yes, it's true his transformation is due in large part to Dr. Frye, protecting him for centuries before he could hold the bond no longer. But Christabel hates the idea of owning anyone, let alone an angel.

"I suppose this means I have to go to London," Christabel says with a sigh. "And our work here must wait."

Dr. Frye does not argue. "Well, I will be here, transposing selkie songs, if you need me. I look forward to your return. I think it will be good of you to get some closure if nothing else."

"Dr. Frye…"

"Do say hello to Ophaniel when you see him."

4

A HIDEOUS PROMONTORY

The memories are the hardest part to endure. They occurred so frequently at first that he wasn't entirely sure he was waking or dreaming. Now, even Ophaniel has trouble keeping them straight from his present, ridiculous, depressing, and altogether *human* existence. So is the difficulty of living eternally. Unlike many angels thrown down from heaven, Ophaniel had the misfortune of falling in love with an Egyptian deity and engendering the wrath of a goddess. And, by extension, his LORD.

Left alone. Shattered. If it hadn't been for that witch finding him centuries ago, he would have died an earthly death.

She—a woman who calls herself Dr. Morgan Frye, who is most certainly not a doctor or a woman—helped him avoid the eye of his enemies long enough that the blood feud dissipated somewhat. He lived for five centuries as a man who transformed into beasts, a Glatisant. It was the rarest of creatures, perhaps rarer than the unicorn. But then he met an actual unicorn and found himself in the Egyptian underground, and before he knew it, he was no longer Worth Goodwin, the Glatisant, but Ophaniel once again.

But now, unlike his years as Worth, when he had friends and lovers, he is utterly alone.

These days, Ophaniel spends a good deal of time in his high apartment, drawing the face of the unicorn. Her name is Christabel, and he has the feeling that he is supposed to love her. That he does love her. That just because he is no longer Worth Goodwin doesn't mean he can simply ignore the feelings he once had. But she comes to see him so rarely. And he doesn't know what to say to her because her eyes are so full of pain that he fears he might weep to watch her any longer. And crying makes him look peaked. And peaked is not a good look on him.

The snake isn't much help, though she at least is consistent. Although Ophaniel appreciates that the snake—Nerissa, her name is Nerissa—has taken him in and allows him space in their building, she does not give him much hope that his life will be anything other than misery, pining, and confusion. Nerissa is a creature of doubt, of cynicism, so it's not surprising that she's of no help. Still, the snake has a companion: the *kitsune*. Ophaniel quite likes Kit, and they have long conversations together since neither of them require much in the way of sleep.

And Kit comes to comfort him during the full moon, when his memories of his dead lover are the worst. Nerissa avoids him then, doubtless because she has lost someone, too. She claims that the bare, silver moon makes her ill. It makes Ophaniel weak, losing his tenuous connection to the celestial realm. But then anger and weakness aren't so different, really. So perhaps they understand each other more fully, would they each open themselves up and allow themselves to be truly vulnerable to one another.

But that is ridiculous.

So, he wallows. And sketches. And complains to himself that he'll be lost forever in this stinking apartment and never again see the face of his LORD.

"I can never get back," he mutters to himself, pacing the sparse room on the top floor of their house on Old Street. "But I should want to go back. Do I want to go back? Some days I don't think I do."

I can't imagine heaven is that good. I mean, they kicked us out and we found our way here and had quite a few adventures. Well, what I mean is that it's been a while. Centuries. No one's come looking. Surely if we're that missed then someone ought to be looking.

It's Worth. The one that Ophaniel was during his imprisonment by the witch's spell. Somehow, even though it's been a decade—which is just a mortal blink, but well enough time to recover for a celestial—he has not been able to shake the creature he once was. Worth exists, not always, but now and again, as a kind of resonance in Ophaniel's head.

And lately, Worth has become more insistent.

Ophaniel sighs, even though he's almost glad that Worth is there. It has been a very lonely time in this grey world since he awoke again. And when the moon is out, it's even worse. But speaking to oneself is perhaps not the ideal method of conversation; still, Ophaniel feels it's better than nothing.

"I'm tired of living on this hideous promontory," Ophaniel says.

It's not a promontory. It's a building. Not even an impressive building. Old Street does have some charms, I've always thought, if you can dig through the dirt. Did you know the poet Keats was born not far from here?

Ophaniel hates it when Worth goes on like this. As if such chatter could ever be interesting to him. What good would knowing the poetry of mortals be, seeing that he has heard the music of Yaweh himself? This Worth, whatever part of him he might be, seems annoyingly connected to such romantic notions.

"Whatever it's called, I don't like it."

The penthouse, if it was even worthy of such a name, is mostly comprised of ugly angles and narrow windows. Ophaniel has done the best he can to keep it clean, which means removing all the unnecessary furniture and retaining only the most essential pieces: a mattress, a chair, and a table. As well as a shelf which Ophaniel does not use for books but rather as a perch (perching being another habit he shares with the *kitsune.*). He doesn't know why, but when he's tired, he very much enjoys sitting up there and looking out across the city. What parts of it he can see, that is. This London place is rather horrible in terms of views. The ever-present fog is like a film before his eyes. But then, there are glimmers when even he, the skeptic of the stars, feels as if perhaps the grime and detritus of the city conceals a power just outside his field of vision; so he keeps trying to steal a glimpse.

You've said that every day for ten years. You'd think that you'd have figured a way out. I'm starting to believe you like these people. They are very kind to you, you know. They have been through a great deal, and the last thing they need in their lives is a whiny, melancholic cherub with a touch of narcissism.

"I'm not narcissistic if I'm genuinely superior to all of those around me."

Case in point. I still hold they're kinder to you than you deserve.

"I'm fairly certain it's because they think you're in me somewhere," Ophaniel mutters, rolling his eyes at his invisible conversant. "Just waiting to be let free. So Ophaniel can die, and everyone else can live happily ever after."

Well, we're talking, aren't we? Doesn't that presuppose that I exist in one form or another?

"That's beside the point."

You never tell them about me. So, they're kind because they're good people.

"They are many things, but good people is not one of them."

Depends on your perspective, I say.

Ophaniel sighs dramatically, batting the air at an invisible foe. "I just keep hoping that you go away."

You're worried that I'm why you can't fly. I told you I can help with that.

Ophaniel is about to growl at the voice in his head, but the floorboards at the top of the stairs are creaking, and that means he's got a visitor. There isn't time to argue with the unwelcome guest in his brain, so he does what is expected and opens the door.

Well, not entirely expected. Ophaniel can open doors—and only doors—telepathically. He must twist his finger just so, and the mechanism obeys and swings open. He doesn't find it odd in the least, but he doesn't remember how or why he should do it; his neighbors find it quite curious.

Flying would be a great deal more impressive. But in the ensuing years, he's lost the ability.

If you let me, I can help you.

It is the snake woman, Nerissa. As she enters the room, she has the same bewildered expression she always has. Except today Ophaniel thinks she might be paler than usual. Her glamour is slipping, and there are scales peeping through at her neck and shadows of her extra limbs if he looks just right. She doesn't make an attractive woman, but he thinks she might be an attractive lamia. He won't tell her this, of course, because he's worried it might go to her head.

"Ophaniel, hello," Nerissa says. It's a polite thing to say, but there is nothing polite about this creature. Ophaniel wishes she wouldn't come to visit him, and the fact she's here in the evening at a time when she's never arrived before is deeply unsettling to him. He is a logical, practical being, and schedules please him greatly. The snake woman is the embodiment of chaos, but until this point, she's been somewhat predictable. "I'm sorry to bother you."

She isn't. She never is.

"Nerissa," Ophaniel says, rolling the r. It sounds better that way, even if no one else pronounces it in such a manner. "Good evening."

"Am I interrupting you?"

It's a stupid question to ask, but Ophaniel bares his teeth in a close approximation of a mortal grin and says, "No. I was merely contemplating the meaning of existence and my place as a fallen celestial unable to commune with their deity. I assure you, whatever concern you have is more pressing than such petty musings."

Nerissa is trying to keep from getting frustrated, and it's one of Ophaniel's favorite states to goad her into. She really does work so hard to keep herself calm, and under the glamour her whole body is roiling with the effort of maintaining her composure. It's rather adorable.

"We've had some news," she says at last. "You see..." There's a letter in her hand, and she fiddles with the edges of it. "We've had a letter. From Beti. Do you remember her? Micheaux delivered it."

Micheaux. Ophaniel shudders inwardly at the name of that walking, perfumed corpse. The day does not appear to be going the direction he'd like it to go. Speaking to Worth was a significant improvement to impending problems. It's been ten years without impending problems. Or at least, any requiring his opinion.

"He's downstairs, isn't he?" Ophaniel sniffs the air.

"Yes, he is. I've told him he may stay the night. But you

see…well, no, you wouldn't see. At the beginning there were glimpses, but now…"

The snake woman is making a sour face, and Ophaniel almost asks if she's got a stomach ailment when he realizes she's crying. All that roiling angst, all that pent-up energy, wasn't fury. It was despair.

He is unprepared for this outpouring of emotion. Nothing makes the angel more uncomfortable than such outward displays of feeling.

"Would you like some tea?" is what he asks. But he does not have tea, does not like tea, and has no actual intention of giving Nerissa tea.

When Nerissa speaks, her voice is hoarse. "You see, it's Vivienne. They've found her."

The name makes a searing sound in his head, and Ophaniel has to stop because Worth starts battering against the edges of his brain, yapping like an insistent shih tzu.

Listen, you fool. It's Vivienne. Listen! This is important!

"She's… she's the one you've been looking for?" Ophaniel hates how his voice sounds. Almost tentative. With none of the holy timbre it ought to have.

Nerissa nods her head slowly, taking a shaky step closer to Ophaniel. She is still far enough away not to offend him too much, but if she gets much closer, he may have more objections.

"I'm going to go to Andalusia. With Micheaux and Kit and Alma. I wanted to know…it's silly to ask, of course, but considering what she meant to Worth." She pauses. "It's going to be dangerous. We've all been looking for her for decades now, and nothing has come up. Leave it to the vampires to find her after all this."

Nerissa lets her words dangle in the air and Ophaniel can do nothing but keep his face still lest he offend her. The snake woman has been good to him; kept him from losing his mind in the beginning, fed him, found answers when Ophaniel had none.

You should go. We should go. Vivienne deserves to know.

"What about the other one?" Ophaniel finally asks. He tries to sound casual but fails miserably. "The odd one. With the funny accent. Is she attending the expedition as well?"

"You mean Christabel?"

"Yes. That one."

"It's not a funny accent. It's an American accent."

"The last time I was walking among mortals, there was no America," he points out.

Christabel won't be there. This is too hard for her. Certainly, you can understand that. She's not like Vivienne, who has seen and loved a thousand times. Christabel is...

"It's doubtful. I did write to her," Nerissa says. "Sent her a telegram yesterday when I got the delivery from Micheaux. But she's deep into her work with Dr. Frye, and I doubt she'll find the time to make the trip."

Ophaniel considers this.

After he takes a little longer than is customary, he proclaims, "I will stay here. I will ensure that no demons come to our doors. Should you need me, you need only call my name."

"Ophaniel. I will be in Andalusia. It's a good deal away from here. It's not like I'll be just downstairs."

"You have saved my life, Nerissa, inasmuch as it is worth. The God of All decreed my name," he explains. "It is written on the lips of the most holy on high. There is power in it for those to whom I grant it."

Nerissa does not seem impressed and gives him a flat expression, her eyes half-lidded, her lips pressed together. "Fine. You stay here. I won't beg this time. We meet at St. Katherine's Docks tomorrow night."

"Why are you telling me that?"

Nerissa sighs. "You know. Just in case you are overcome by a compunction to bless us with your celestial effluvium."

The cherub doesn't have anything more to say and isn't surprised when Nerissa turns sharply on her heel and leaves. It's true that he has nothing better to do, but he doesn't like to look desperate to the non-celestials. How could they possibly understand what it feels like to be someone like him?

You're making a poor choice, Ophaniel. In many ways. These people are the only key to you ever getting your wings. The world has changed so much since you fell...and I won't help you if you don't help them.

5

SWAN SONG

Vivienne never was afraid of darkness. As a night creature, a sylph with centuries of experience mulling about dimly lit forests and haunted ruins, the dark was a symbol of comfort and strength. She used to think that she could see better in the dark, discern the true from the false more clearly. After the tragic turns of her youth, darkness became a refuge, a balm to her soul.

Vivienne understands there is something worse than darkness.

Bastille is a creature of the void. Not of darkness. Vivienne laughed when he told her this the first time, thinking it some strange joke. In her mind, there were two primary poles in the world of supernatural beings: creatures of the day and creatures of the night. Some become good; some become evil. Others never really left to their own choices. But one's affinity for sunlight has little to do with it.

But the void is a category unto itself, reserved for beings who have gone far beyond "good" and "bad" and straight into delusion. Except in that delusion is power.

Bastille is a *basilisk*, but that is the least of his unfortunate qualities. He possesses many of the charms of his kind: the ability to transform from man to creature, the presence of poisonous fangs, the capacity to turn people and objects to stone. These do not put him above and beyond the monsters of the world.

As Vivienne has learned these twenty years, Bastille is a priest of the void. She has discovered this not by asking after for such knowledge, but rather because he tells her frequently. Once she figured out he had no desire for her body and he just wanted to soliloquize, the captivity was at least a bit less stressful. But no less boring.

"I am one among few remaining who adhere to an old, old faith known to spring from the oldest of sources," he has said on many an occasion. "There was not only light and dark in the beginning. There was the *absence*—a chaotic vacuum of a void where great power awaited. Perhaps I am not the highest priest, but I am the most loyal. So many have fallen by the wayside, but I have remained Cygna's most trustworthy ally. Her Chosen."

Cygna.

Vivienne has never seen Cygna, but Nadine has. Nadine, the ifrit—and truly Vivienne's only friend—similarly fell afoul of Barqan ages ago.

"The Circle of Iapetus was our idea, of course," Bastille has told her repeatedly. "We didn't expect it to actually work. We were feeding them information. We needed the energy collected by that creature in New York to work as a kind of guide-star for our work. And lo and behold, under the rock came skittering you and your ridiculous friends. Barqan got his freedom, and we got so much more than we bargained for."

Except Christabel. They have still not managed to locate the unicorn, and not for lack of trying.

So, now it has been twenty years, and still Vivienne has

not seen Cygna, but has heard her name thousands of times in Bastille's long monologues on his importance. Which of course means that he's rather unimportant in the grand scheme, and that makes Vivienne even a bit more bitter; she is held captive by a moron.

She has tried to learn more about this Cygna, but other than speaking her name as one does a goddess, Bastille gives nothing away. Sometimes Vivienne doesn't believe she exists at all. For who could? She does not seem to be monstrous in any measure, or at least Nadine says time and again that there is nothing particularly notable about the woman that she can remember. No extra legs. No powers. Not so much as a pair of mismatched eyes. But then Nadine has a difficult time telling the difference between most humanoids. She claims that those without fire in their veins look dull to her.

And now they are in Andalusia. Vivienne knows she has been here before, but in one of her other lives. It's how she makes sense of her long existence. She was not always as she is now; she's had to reinvent herself. But she has been Vivienne du Lac the longest, and as she stands, she is the closest to herself as she can be.

Or she was once. Now, Vivienne lives without her magic. The metal about her wrists dampens her powers to the point that summoning even a single snowflake would be near impossible.

So, Vivienne seems to spend most of her time tidying things, and while at first that was a rather mortifying experience she has since found a kind of solace in the hard work. Since she cannot use any of her abilities, she has had to rely on the cleverness of her hands. She cleans, she mends, and from time to time, she creates. Though it is much more difficult sewing by hand, she has found pride in the clothing she has designed for Bastille and the other inhabitants of his ever-moving house.

And now the villa looks somewhat presentable. Far be it from her to welcome Cygna, but if she is coming, Vivienne at least does not want to be responsible for a slovenly abode.

"What do you suppose she wants with the master?" Nadine asks, combing her long fingers through her hair. Her skin is still kindled, but she cannot strike out in defense. Bastille is always frustrated that he hasn't yet deduced a method to dim her entirely, and he has gone through at least six collars trying to do so.

"I wouldn't know," Vivienne says through the needle between her teeth. She is giving Nadine her last fitting in the presentation dress she'll have for Cygna's arrival. Unlike Vivienne, Nadine is considered essential staff.

Outfitting the ifrit is no simple task. The first two dresses ended up singed beyond recognition, and Vivienne had to start from scratch. Nadine emits constant heat, a blue flame. It does marvelous things for her hair and eyes, providing a kind of blazing ripple about her skin and features. In fact, Vivienne finds that any clothing is superfluous on the ifrit, but that is not her decision.

So Nadine must wear an elegant dress made of intricately sewn metallic hoops, put together with silver floss, hardened leather, and wax-coated muslin. She does not burn hot enough to concern Vivienne with this combination of materials, but earlier in the process, she lost a great deal of work to spontaneous combustion.

"You look lovely," Vivienne says, walking the ifrit in front of the mirror. It takes a moment for Nadine's body to appear in the reflection, some strange delay she always has, but the result is rather breathtaking. The long, narrow dress falls to the ifrit's bare feet, deeply cut in the front and back. This ingenious material, so Vivienne is proud enough to admit, looks almost like silk from a distance, adding a sumptuous, liquid presentation.

Nadine smiles, each tooth flecked with dancing flame. "You are far too kind, considering everything."

"It is my duty," Vivienne says, holding up her hands in silent resign. "But, for what it's worth, I did find the process rather enjoyable, if not frustrating at times."

Nadine closes her eyes a moment, in a motion that Vivienne has learned to interpret as a blush. When did this flirtation begin? Vivienne can't remember. She tells herself it is merely a coping mechanism in this difficult place, and that perhaps she's just getting desperate. But Vivienne finds every flicker and tongue of fire on Nadine perfect.

If only she could see her in her full glory.

Vivienne has had many lovers over her long life, but very few women. Given Nerissa's constant mooning over her, she had honestly considered it just not part of her own personal spectrum. Until Nadine, and her fire skin, and her voice like hushed velvet, and her nearly unquenchable fire.

Nadine has a story; Vivienne is sure of it. Bastille made mention more than a few times that though Barqan is a king of the djinn, Nadine once held significantly more power. That is why she has two collars and two pairs of bangles at her wrists and legs. That is why she is not entirely dampened.

But Vivienne has not asked more. At first because of their strained relationship, but now the sylph is afraid to risk whatever they have by making Nadine uncomfortable.

For Vivienne's part, she wears what is expected and no more. A long pale grey veil pinned back on her slick black hair; her body draped in soft layers of tulle. In the old days, she would have woven it from spider silk. Now, and without time to spend on her own presentation, she must make do with local silk. A simple hammered silver belt adorns her waist. She has never needed much in the way of ornamentation. But without access to her charms, she is somewhat diminished. The layers of silk help mask her emaciated form, her sinewy arms. She is fed but not nourished here.

"Vivienne," Nadine says.

Vivienne looks up from her sewing kit, double-checking that she has accounted for all the pieces. Once she lost a pair of scissors, and she was made to pay the price by being cut down the inside of her leg with Bastille's claws. The infection and fever didn't kill her, but they did serve as a reminder not to lose track of the gifts he'd given her—if they could be called so.

"Yes, Nadine?"

"Thank you," says the ifrit in her soft, hushed voice. "I know this is not where either of us imagined we'd be. And with Cygna coming I...I don't know what will happen."

"Oh, it's nothing. In this dreadful place, I take what joy I can. And making you look the royalty you are is no challenge."

"It's only that I wanted to say..."

"Alas, my molars are aching, and that means I'm late for the master," Vivienne says, skirting by the ifrit toward the door.

Nadine takes just a moment to brush her fingers across Vivienne's face as she exits, the touch like a hot wind. Vivienne shudders against it, the full power of her desire still muted. She grits her teeth.

"I will see you this evening," Vivienne says, and makes her way out, averting her eyes. She can feel Nadine's own gaze upon her as she leaves, questioning and full of fire.

Cygna is set to arrive at seven, and so Vivienne makes the slow progression toward Bastille's wing of the house a little past six. He is quite precise about presentation and timing, the definitions of which seem to change with whatever suits him.

Bastille is sitting outside on the terrace, the shadows of

vines falling across his angular face, waiting for her. As usual, Vivienne marvels at his beauty, his ageless features masterfully drawn. But then he turns his face to observe her, and the coldness in his eyes feels like iron on her skin.

Standing slowly, Bastille folds his arms across his chest, tilting his head just so to appraise his possession. Vivienne has to remind herself that he has never done anything untoward with her outside of corporal punishment, though he's had many the opportunity. She cannot recall a single time that he even put a hand on her, or even threatened ravishment. And yet the way he looks at her always feels a violation.

"Are you eating enough, sylph?"

The words are sharp, disapproving.

"Yes, Lord Bastille. I am eating what is given," Vivienne says.

"Can you not put some rouge on your cheeks?" Bastille draws a little closer to Vivienne, examining her face. "You look mottled. Like a corpse. Are you a corpse? I confess I don't know what a 'sylph' really is. Just a general term, isn't it?"

Vivienne replies, "I am a sylph. Perhaps there was another word long ago for what I am, but I have forgotten it." Which is not exactly true, but not exactly false either. "And with the rouge—I have tried. But something about my skin absorbs any attempt. I think it's likely, well, you know. I am a cold-natured thing."

"A shame," Bastille says. "Cygna certainly expects more than...well, whatever it is you are. But then, she may be too concerned with important matters to notice. Still, keep your face veiled, will you? I will not have my servants looking like half-dead mortals."

"Yes, Lord," Vivienne says. She feels the sting of his words while simultaneously scolding herself for such an emotion.

For most of her long, long life, Vivienne has gone through her daily adventures with a keen understanding that she is the loveliest person in any given room. But since her imprisonment, she has diminished greatly.

What Nerissa would think of her now.

Nerissa.

There is not a day that goes by that Vivienne regrets how she dealt with her oldest and best friend. That Nerissa fell in love with her was unfortunate. But Vivienne knows she should have seen it coming, knows she should have expected it. Still, if she had paid more attention to Nerissa and not to her own reflection, she might have figured out the whole business with Barqan earlier. This entire mess is her doing, brought to pass by her pride.

At least the lamia has stopped looking for her. Vivienne risked everything to reach out to Nerissa through the masks she'd been making for Bastille during their time in Cairo, gathering elements needed for his grand plan. Ever since, she's been relegated to more prosaic tasks—none of them leaving the walls of the facility. But it was worth it. Even with the flaying. Her body healed, as it always did. Just not as fast as it used to.

Vivienne manages to keep going because she knows her friends—Worth and Nerissa and even that annoying young unicorn Christabel—are safe.

A half-hour later and the entire house staff is standing at attention in the center courtyard. They are a ragtag bunch, mostly cuffed and dampened, a mismatched mélange of dwarves, nymphs, satyrs, a *kappa*, and two vampires. There is a table set with lavish food; one of the nymphs plays a soft panpipe in the background. Nadine looks resplendent, her gown quite literally outshining the rest.

Vivienne is just starting to get uncomfortable with the waiting when she hears Bastille's clear voice.

"Ah, here she is."

Bastille is looking toward the center of the room, but Vivienne can't see anything of note. There are a few hushed murmurs from the staff.

"Welcome, Cygna. We, your devoted servants, are honored by your presence."

It may be the veil, or more likely her shackles, but for a moment it does appear as if Bastille is speaking into a void of nothingness.

But that is it, isn't it?

Out of nothing, and Vivienne cannot understand exactly how she knows it's *nothing* since it is not dark and it is not visible, a woman unfolds. She is not winged, not even caped, but coming through this slice of nothing in the world of *not nothing*, Cygna unfurls. The pieces of her body rearrange themselves: a head, broad shoulders, a compact frame. Her hair is short and curled, the color of a grey sky, the hue matching her eyes.

The rest of Cygna is, how can Vivienne comprehend such a strange thing, unapologetically un-magical. She wears mortal clothes, cut in the current Western fashion. She carries a briefcase. She wears Oxfords with a Spanish heel. Her hat has a white feather in it, and even Vivienne can tell her tailor is Parisian.

"Bastille," Cygna says. "At last. It's been too long."

Nadine pulls on Vivienne's sleeve and widens her eyes, hissing, "Kneel."

Every nerve in Vivienne's body recoils at the thought. Kneel to this woman? Kneel to anyone? Twenty years ago, Vivienne would have given the woman a long telling to. But now Vivienne is acutely aware of something she never had to worry about in her previous life: pain. The pain has changed her, rearranged her bones, taken hope and power from her very center.

And so she bows, watching out of the corner of her eye as Bastille does the same.

"Well, it's good to see people know their places around here," Cygna says, her voice smooth as honey and tinged with just a little roughness. It's a lovely voice. But it brings a chill.

When no one makes an answer, Cygna says, "Now, which one do we flay first?"

6

THE BLEAKNESSES

The mere idea of sailing on the open sea is enough to slow Nerissa considerably on her path toward St. Katherine's docks. That, and she is worried she hasn't packed enough implet. She's checked three times already, but now she's second-guessing her math.

Regardless of her food supplies, Alma will be waiting for her at the docks, and that is somewhat comforting. And Beti, the vampire and Micheaux's matron has promised to speak with them as well. But that does nothing to alleviate the dread of an inevitable sea voyage. The last ten years have given Nerissa a reprieve from travel, and nothing is worse than a ship out in the open. Except perhaps an airplane. But she refuses even to consider that option.

It is difficult to fall too far behind, however, because Kit is brimming with excitement so fully and inappropriately that she's beginning to garner attention from passers-by. So, Nerissa quickens her pace while cursing her companion under her breath. The last thing she wants is Kit running amok in London again. There are too many distractions and shiny objects, to say nothing of the unsavory underbits which so preternaturally draw Kit. The last time she went on a London journey, it took Nerissa six washes to get the stink out of Kit's tail.

Nerissa once hoped that a time of quiet and ritual might do well to temper the *kitsune*, but on the contrary, Kit is more ebullient than ever. Pent up, even. While Kit may have more hobbies—including knitting, archery, and occult arts—she is nonetheless a magnet for adventure. Though the old snake would be lying to herself if she said she didn't enjoy having Kit around, at least a little. Especially the flush of her cheeks when she is in a genuinely mischievous mood. And the light on her eyes when the moon is full. And the curve of her tails when she…

The docks bustle with the evening crowd, a constant din of human calls and cries flitting around them as incessantly as the gulls. It smells of fish guts and sweaty man bodies, and Nerissa has to take a discreet sip of her implet to give her resolve. It is not often she gets the desire to rip relentlessly into human bodies, sating herself on their moist, salty blood; but something about the combination of commerce and testosterone tends to put her in the mood.

Nerissa is nervous, doing her best to avoid the complicated emotions regarding Vivienne—the sylph who spurned her twenty years ago and then abruptly got herself kidnapped—and she doesn't quite notice the little figure beckoning her until she's almost trampled it underfoot.

It's a child. But it is also a corpse. A vampire child. It has limpid green eyes in a smudged face, eerily long fingernails, and a pair of crooked spectacles that look as if they do nothing more than make a strange fashion statement.

"This way," says the vampire child. "Mistress is waiting for you."

Miraculously, Kit has doubled back and slides up to Nerissa with practiced ease. The *kitsune* links her arm through Nerissa's with such familiarity that Nerissa is no longer nervous about Vivienne-related emotions and briefly can concentrate only on the pressure between them.

"What a strange little creature," Kit says as they take a winding route through the dwindling crowd. "It's rather lopsided for a vampire, don't you think?"

Kit is not good at whispering, and the little vampire turns around with a sly grin but says nothing more.

"Oh, Kit. Not every vampire is symmetrical. It's rude to point out their inequities. They already are so low on the rung of monsters," Nerissa says.

"The office is this way," the vampire says, pointing to a gap between two buildings. "Mistress is waiting for you."

"Oh good," Nerissa says, taking in the view. Kit has still not removed her arm from Nerissa's, and the lamia is having a tough time keeping her emotional armor up. Not that Kit has never shown affection or recognition, only that this time it feels different. Protective. Fond. "Curious that all our contacts never seem to have proper addresses."

The little vampire gurgles something incomprehensible, then beckons them forward. They limp as if they've been struck, and now that Nerissa thinks about it, perhaps Kit is right.

"Is this vampire familiar to you?" Nerissa asks.

"No, why?" Kit tilts her head toward Nerissa, her nose wrinkling just a second. "It smells like all vampires smell. Dead. This one is just a crooked dead."

As she's been in many similar situations before, parading head-first into nefarious and highly suspicious locations, Nerissa is not surprised by the narrow door that opens with a click from the little vampire. Nor is she taken aback when they have to wind their way down a long, twisting corridors. She also doesn't stop to question the musty smell, the guttering light from the torches, or the general medieval look and feel of the place.

But the ghost.

The ghost is surprising.

Though human lore is full of ghost sightings, Nerissa has found that they are either far rarer than believed or simply adverse to interaction with supernatural creatures like herself. In the hundreds of years since her birth, she has never encountered a ghost, and so she startles at the sight before her.

The ghost presents as a woman of middling years, not transparent exactly, but limned in purplish-grey light. The apparition is very keenly dressed, and Nerissa gets the sense her finery isn't an illusion. She is actually wearing clothes, but they have somehow avoided deterioration for the better part of a...what, half millennia? If Vivienne were here, she would know precisely the century to which this woman belongs, what with her wimple and her long, thick gown. She'd probably recognize the handiwork down to the specific artisan. But fashion blurs together in Nerissa's long memory so she cannot decipher Tudor from Regency.

The ghost smiles.

"Is she here?" the little vampire asks. It sounds afraid.

Kit's eyes fill with the light of refracted stars as she stares, her mouth parted slightly. "I see a miracle," the *kitsune* says softly. "Or, more properly, a vision I can only ascribe to miracles. It is a walking ancestor, unfettered by the chains of the world. Oh, glorious. She's glorious!"

"You see it, too, then?" Nerissa holds Kit's arm tighter.

"I can't see," the little vampire sighs, slicking back its long, pale hair. "But I know how to get through. Mistress told me."

The specter smiles placidly at Nerissa and then at Kit. Then she speaks in a voice that seems to come from all corners of the room. No, from the very stones themselves.

"You may address me as Her Royal Highness, Queen Phillippa of England," says the ghost without a trace of irony. "Welcome to St. Katharine's Hospital."

Nerissa knows enough of general London history to remember that St. Katharine's Hospital is long gone, along with the abbey that was once here. She visited the place, long ago, and enjoyed a most satisfying meal of plump monks out gathering herbs by the Thames. They tasted of malt. And watercress. A lovely combination. That was another life, though, and she ought to be repentant about it. And she is. Mostly.

"Your Royal Highness," Kit says immediately, though she does not bow. She, as ever, remains unmoved by the doings of men. "You are a lovely being, and we are so fortunate to see you."

Queen Phillippa does not smile at this, but she nods slightly, looking at Nerissa narrowly. "Have I seen you before?"

"I doubt it," Nerissa says, though that is a possibility. "We are simply seeking passage through your...ah, hospital?" She immediately regrets the rise in her voice at the end. Ghosts, she has heard, are easily confused.

"You have very sharp teeth," Phillippa says, frowning down into her high collar, looking even more deeply at Nerissa. "But you won't be able to bite your way through. I guard this passage, and I decide who gets to go through."

Nerissa examines the walls. Yes, she can sense a bit of Geist magic interlaced among the stones. Even though the hospital is gone, it's clear Philippa has managed to weave her own power into the passageway. And indeed, when Nerissa tries to take a step forward, she's met by a solid resistance though there's nothing but air.

"You see?" The Queen gives them a sweet grin. "I am

ancient, and you must placate me." Then she giggles. "I do like sounding so fearsome."

The little vampire pulls on Nerissa's jacket. "Give it this. Mistress says it likes books."

Nerissa feels a little book in her hand and pulls it dimly to her face. She does not have her spectacles on, but she can tell it's a precious creation. An illuminated manuscript, a book of hours, if she's right on her history. Christabel would know more details. Where would a vampire get it? And, moreover, how could a vampire even hold it?

She frowns a little. Perhaps this vampire is too young to concern themselves with religious artifacts...but still.

Glancing at Kit, Nerissa makes a desperate expression. This is the way to Vivienne; what other choice have they? If Beti is within, either she managed another entrance or had another book.

Nerissa feels tired, worried. But the *implet* is leaving her systems and, along with it, her senses; regardless of Kit's progressively concerned appearance, Nerissa agrees.

"I have a book," Nerissa says. "For our passage beyond."

"Yes, I will trade you," says Phillippa, her voice bright and musical. She holds up her hands and the book she was holding moments ago now rises with her motions, drifting across the space between them.

Nerissa tries the same, but her book fails to catch the magical tide, and so Kit picks up the book and hands it gently to Queen Phillippa as Nerissa opens the book for trade.

It is a small thing, this tome, and heavy for its size. Christabel will know what to do with it. It's a bestiary of some sort. As soon as Nerissa runs her fingers over the cover, though, Phillippa disappears into the walls surrounding them. The whole stonework around them shimmers that same purplish hue that so recently emanated from the Queen.

Nerissa is not surprised when the little vampire tries to grab the book from her, and even less surprised when Kit pins the creature up against the wall.

"I don't like being used," Nerissa says, quickly storing the book in her pocket, and feeling for her *implet* at the same time. The cold glass under her fingertips is calming and reassuring—a counterpoint to the fury rising in her.

Never trust vampires.

"I'm sorry. Mistress said—" the little vampire gurgles under Kit's clutches. The *kitsune*'s nails are out, her slick black hair rising around her as her power manifests.

"Apologies are dust," Kit says, pressing her face closer to the vampire. "Explain yourself, little wriggling creature of death and decay."

Nerissa stifles a smile. Kit always has the most endearing name for monsters even when she's interrogating them.

"We can't...we can't see ghosts..." gasps the vampire.

"Yes? And?" Nerissa walks a little closer, examining the passageway before and behind them. She can smell salt air. So at least the vampire was leading her in the right direction.

"She wanted the book," the vampire says. "Mistress wanted the book."

"Well, she'll have to ask nicely," says Nerissa. "Now, tiny vampire. Show us the way to Beti. Hopefully, Micheaux will meet us there, and we can chalk it all up to a misunderstanding. I have quite a lot to say about Beti's surprisingly bad taste in messengers."

"Nerissa..." Kit is about to say something long-winded and detailed, but Nerissa is having none of it at the moment.

"We don't have time to waste, Kit," replies the lamia. "We'll handle whatever comes our way. We always do."

* * *

Beti is there waiting for them in an immense cavern, cut out of the side of what must have been the hospital's foundation. There is a sandy beach, a little pier, and then, around the corner, a boat.

These are all good details, but Nerissa can see that Beti is not well. It has been nearly a decade since the last time Nerissa saw Beti, the rather humble-looking coven queen of Cairo, but the vampire looks wan and withered. And that's saying something for a vampire who, in Nerissa's experience, rarely look better than a barely cold corpse. She has a greedy, desperate look in her eyes when Nerissa and Kit emerge into the cave, but her features do not betray her emotions.

"Beti," Nerissa says, not letting go of the small vampire. "We found your emissary. We expected a peaceful transition, but I'm a bit confused with your lack of care. Bartering with a ghost? Stealing?"

Beti does not smile but shakes her head sadly. "So, you see the state of our affairs," she says. "Murmur. I told you to be careful."

The vampire shudders under Nerissa's hand. "I was tired. I was hungry. They would not give me the book."

"Did you bring us here under false pretenses, Beti?" Nerissa takes a step forward, tossing Murmur forward. The vampire staggers and almost falls, but rights itself before tumbling. "We've had a long peace between us. We've welcomed Micheaux into our home countless times. We've relied on you."

What she's really thinking is that if she severs her relationship with the vampires, how is she going to get her *implet*? That anger tinges her voice more than any general concern.

The cavern is eerily quiet save their voices. Nerissa

notices how her speech reverberates across the water, sending echoes, like answering whispers, around the small enclosure. The Thames is just beyond. Their ticket to Vivienne…

"I am a desperate creature," Beti says, holding out her hands as if it explains everything. Her voice, though. It isn't right?

"Where is Micheaux?" Kit asks.

Beti shakes her head as if dispelling a bad dream. "I have sent him away. I do not think he is impartial enough any longer to remain in my employ. But nor are you impartial. I believe that celestial has corrupted your mind. You are not seeing clearly. I was merely asking a favor of you, not trying to steal. It was simply good timing, especially considering the information I so freely gave on the subject of Vivienne du Lac."

Nerissa knows this is not the way Beti speaks. It may be her body, but there is another force behind her eyes.

Best not to let her know yet, though. Not with her entire food supply at risk.

"As I asked a favor of you ten years ago," Nerissa says, taking a step closer toward Beti, watching to see the vampire's reaction. She does not flinch. "Did you think I had forgotten? That I would not give you something you sought if you had asked? But duplicitousness does not become you. I have always been open with you and gave my home to Micheaux when he needed it."

Murmur is acting curiously now as Beti speaks. Twitching. Eyes moving strangely.

"It is not a matter…not a matter of…" Beti, who Nerissa no longer truly believes is Beti at all, shivers. "Not a matter of…ugh, demons, he's here."

There is a curious light about the place. For such a dank

cavern, Nerissa finds that she can suddenly see much better. And she smells a familiar scent, like hot rocks after a rain.

Ophaniel. Nerissa turns to look at him, and realizes her mistake too late.

Beti, or the creature she has become, is on Nerissa quicker than she can quite comprehend. The lamia reaches up to meet a blow from Beti, rending the vampire's hand with her claws as it comes down.

The flesh parts like paper.

Slowly, the being within, a creature of darkness and ash, emerges from the shell of Beti's body. It is not dark so much as it is *empty*, a void within the darkness of the cavern, like a hole punched through the heart of the universe. But very, very much alive.

"Drink the void," says the voice. "Before it drinks you."

7

MISSED EXITS

Kit knows the *ten no tsukai* is on the way before Nerissa does, but that's not unusual. It's one of the reasons Kit stays along with the snake woman. She likes her. She values her. She protects her. Kit does not want bad things to happen to her, even if Nerissa is far too reliant on that glittering imp ichor she drinks and has the habit of sulking all the time.

It feels like love sometimes. But then Kit thinks, no. It feels like the need to protect. Not that Nerissa is incapable of taking care of herself. She is a creature built from violence, even though she has learned to temper it.

It's only...

Kit wouldn't be able to forgive herself if anything terrible happens to Nerissa. The thought is like ice in her veins.

And she doesn't trust the *ten no tsukai* that was once her friend named Worth. Not that Ophaniel is an evil creature; no, Kit has learned in her many long years of life that good and evil are not so easily distinguished on first glance. Or indeed after successive glances. She just feels as if the *ten no tsukai* is hiding secrets and knowledge. Important knowledge that would help bring Nerissa's lost friend Vivienne to them. Or at least that he could perhaps be more helpful than sitting and complaining about everything all day long.

But it's good that Ophaniel appears and Kit cannot help but be a little glad. He is a glimmering form of feathers and skin the color and texture of marble—really not so glamorous as one might think—and as soon as he shouts, the void creatures that were once the vampires begin to vibrate.

Kit has never liked vampires, but she should have been more aware when the little one started acting funny. It was hard to smell it, what with all the saltwater and fish and the refuse from the day's trading. And the fact they were wrapped in corpse skin. Vampires smell like corpses. She just hadn't checked deeper. Nerissa's behavior was bothering her; she was becoming addicted to the *implet*. But every time Kit tried to broach the subject…

In the conversations she's had with him, Kit has learned that Ophaniel can no longer fly, but he can extend his wings. As a celestial, he is able to bend light to his will. It's not that he emanates light exactly, but he can manipulate light in any circumstance. Even in a dim cavern. He pulses one, two, three times, and the void monsters shiver again against the illumination. They don't like it, and that's good.

Kit must step around the discarded vampire skins, wincing as she slips in one of them, as she positions herself against the smaller shape. She doesn't hesitate. This is when the joy comes in, when her absolute appreciation of her being courses through her.

But it is much more difficult when one can't quite see their prey. The emptiness that is—or was—the little vampire called Murmur appears to appear and disappear around her, defying even the physics of monster magic. Kit's only aid is Ophaniel's light-bending. Where the light hits the emptiness, it turns an off-white that reminds her of dusty mold from mushrooms.

The longer they fight, the less human-shaped the once-vampires become. Nonetheless, Ophaniel's light helps, and for now, they outnumber the void monsters, so it's time for fun.

Kit lets loose her shriek, which is both very like a woman screaming and much worse, or so she has been told. The cry reverberates in the close quarters, and as the sound waves return to her she shivers and extends her tails. She now has five. She's very proud of the fifth one, but she isn't quite used to the balance, and she hesitates.

Pain lashes her, right across the back. That second of lost balance and the little shit of a once-vampire hits her so hard she sees stars. It feels like she's propelling forward into nothing for a heart-wrenching second, time and space melding about her, but then she is standing, winded, sweating, clammy. Kit has never felt *clammy* in her entire life.

Shaking her head to get her bearings, Kit tries to flank the creature with Nerissa, who has now gone full snake. Normally, Kit likes to admire Nerissa when she's like that—her glossy scales, the yellow flash of her eyes, the color of her blood-red lips, and those glorious, muscled arms—but there is no time for beautiful distractions, even if she aches for it. Even if she…

Kick. Bite. Rend. It is so hard to make any of these basic attacks when the assailants have no physical form that she can determine. In fact, Kit feels a subtle pull from them as they get closer, some strange gravitational current. What madness? She doesn't want to go closer to them, and yet her body seems to have other plans.

"Kit, you holding up?" Nerissa is breathless. Tired. She tried encircling the once-vampire with her tail, but that didn't work.

"I'm here," Kit says.

The *ten no tsukai* is not helping much, aside from his general light-bending which, while useful, doesn't do much to *stop* the violent creatures. Even when Kit is hitting them, her attacks aren't doing much in the way of damage.

It is not going well.

Kit catches Nerissa's eyes, her brilliant golden eyes, and she sees the same fear that beats in her own heart. It does not seem fair that they would perish here, not with such an unnamable darkness, not so far from everything. Not so close to Vivienne… if that's what Nerissa truly wants…

The bleakness—yes, that is what she will call them—smothers Kit, both pressing down on her and pulling her deeper into its emptiness. It was so small before, and now it seems like an endless expanse, an ever-growing nothing.

She hits the stone floor of the cavern hard, so hard that she gags on her tongue. Her teeth seek blood, contact, anything, but it is like fighting the wind, a vaguely sucking wind.

Kit's strength begins to wane. She has never felt a sensation so strange in her life, and she has been licked by a goat on her…

Who was she, again? She forgets her name.

What was she thinking? She will never need to remember again.

Yes, the bleakness. A soft, cold velveteen dissolution into…

Just when Kit is about to turn herself over to the bleakness, she becomes acutely aware of Nerissa standing between her and her quarry. The lamia is alternating between yelling and hissing, her scales dappled in the dim light, but oh so beautiful.

Kit is positive Nerissa is fighting, but she still can't quite shake the existential dread.

Until a sickly, snapping noise rouses her, that is, and the lamia lets out a scream so deafening the cavern itself trembles. Kit feels it in her teeth.

Kit slowly wipes dirt and a sticky substance from her eyes, burning and blurring her vision. What in the world is happening? Is the earth shaking?

No, it's Alma. The dwarf with the maggot white skin and the clear eyes. The one that can grow back her limbs—albeit slowly—like a skink. She's come up through the ground as she is wont to do, and while the smaller of the bleaknesses is gone, the larger one is no longer attacking Ophaniel because the dwarf is filling its maw with as many rocks as possible. Bricks, pebbles, boulders, they all come to the ground as easily as if they were rising through water.

"Yes, almost there!" Ophaniel is laughing, grinning, clapping his hands. Blood has splattered his face—who is bleeding?—and he looks livelier than Kit has ever seen him. "Keep the onslaught of rocks on, dwarf woman!"

Kit slips before she stands, just in time to hear a crack like nearby thunder and watch the larger bleakness vanish. Or, rather, simply leave. For how can a being already possessed of negative matter cease to be? Relief floods her body, and she shivers as if with new life.

She is almost ready to celebrate when she notices Nerissa. The lamia is on her knees, breathing heavy, cradling her right arm, ragged words tumbling from her with no coherence. She is in her human glamour, mostly. Which is strange.

Taking a few steps forward, her legs still far from compliant, the picture comes into view. It's Nerissa's right side. Or what remains of it from outside the glamour. From the elbow down it is…nothing.

Doing some mental calculation, Kit realizes that if she'd lost one arm of her glamoured self, then that would make two of her true body…

"Shit and limestone." That is from Alma. "I'm going to check the perimeter!"

"Nerissa!"

Kit shouts Nerissa's name a thousand times louder than she should have. Enough that both the *ten no tsukai* and the dwarf look at her sharply.

Before she considers the propriety of it, Kit has Nerissa in her arms, kissing her forehead. The lamia is in pain beyond measure and Kit can feel it through her skin. It is colder than she had thought, but not unlovely.

"Oh, oh, I need to help," Kit hears herself saying, her voice distant. "Does the *ten no tsukai*, I mean, Ophaniel…"

"I am fine; I am…" The *ten no tsukai* does not offer anything else. He, too, stares at Nerissa.

Nerissa is not fine. Nothing is fine. It will never be fine ever again. With a shudder, the lamia lets go of her glamor completely, utterly, casting aside what hints of humanity she has carried with her so long. Kit notices the subtle shifting of color on Nerissa's scales, the varying size and pattern down her neck, the way even swirls and lines cover her lips . Nerissa's hair is black and sleek, silky soft beneath Kit's fingers. She wants to kiss every strand. She wants to apologize for sometimes being annoying and demanding, for sulking and not saying what she should have said and instead filling up every bit of air with useless words.

And for failing to protect her.

She should have protected Nerissa. She should have fought off the bleaknesses. Kit's tears fall on Nerissa's face, the water filling the gaps between her scales and then vanishing.

But it is not magic.

The bleaknesses took two of Nerissa's arms. Snapped them off like the claws of a crab.

"She's dying…" Kit whispers. "Her body is shaking. She's

59

lost a great deal of blood, and though her blood is not the only part of her keeping her alive, as she has a most complex limbic system that works as a kind of secondary circulatory track…"

Then there is a face before her, grabbing her by the chin, stopping her blubbering.

Ophaniel materializes before her through a haze of tears and Kit startles. Yet, when she looks up into his face, she doesn't see the alien lines, those cold marks she has noted on so many occasions. No, it is a familiar face. Mostly. Also, still the *ten no tsukai.*

Worth Goodwin.

"Worth?" Nerissa whispers.

"I'm going to check the exits," Alma says, sinking back down into the ground like a burrowing worm. Normally, the dwarf's strange method of moving through soil and rock bothers Kit, but at the moment she is too engulfed with the overwhelming dread that she might lose Nerissa.

"Hush, friend," Worth says, though he is somehow speaking through the *ten no tsukai.* Ophaniel/Worth—Kit is as confused as anyone—is most assuredly winged and naked, among other improprieties, but the voice is familiar. "Take a deep breath."

Worth leans down and puts a long-fingered hand on Nerissa's chest, just below her collar bone. A low blue light emanates from his fingertips, then soaks into the lamia's body like Kit's tears.

Nerissa shudders.

"I appear to be…missing my arm… arms…?" Nerissa makes a barking noise that might be a laugh, but Kit thinks she's just trying not to cry. "I'm sorry. I knew…something was… wrong…"

Talking is clearly laborious, and Kit tries to tell Nerissa to be quiet, but she's also afraid that if she makes herself more obvious, the lamia will notice Kit holding her and stroking her long, silky hair. And she does not want to stop doing that.

"We've got you, Nerissa Waldemar," Worth says. "Now take a deep breath. I'm going to apply some pressure, and it'll feel a lot better. Kit, get me that vile stuff she's been drinking. I'd normally not advise using it—she already uses it too often —but in this case, we need her alert."

"I can hear you," Nerissa hisses. "I'm not...dead yet..."

Kit doesn't know why she's crying more; because Nerissa is in pain or because she's hearing Worth's voice again. Either way, she steels herself. She must. This isn't going to be pretty.

"An astute observation, as expected," Worth says.

"We're going to miss the boat," Nerissa mutters, craning her head to look in the direction they were going. She gasps in pain as Worth, or a close approximation of him, peels off some of the material at the elbow. He whispers his apologies.

"You're not being metaphorical, are you?" Worth gives a shy glance at Kit. "She's not. There is an actual boat. I... almost remember."

Kit wants to ask him a thousand questions—how is he here again? Where has he been? Where is Ophaniel?—but she's incapable of speaking at the moment. She and Nerissa have faced down their fair share of strange creatures, but never has Nerissa been beaten so swiftly and so completely.

But sitting silent is not going to help matters.

"There was a boat," Kit says slowly, shaking off the numbness of seeing Nerissa in so much pain, but also realizing what this will mean. "It came here from Andalusia. We think Vivienne was on it, or at least someone might have been on it who could show us the way. But now it's unlikely we'll make the boat at all, let alone find this Vivienne."

Both Nerissa and Worth look at Kit sharply.

"I mean your Vivienne?" Kit tries again.

Alma has returned now, in that strange silent way of hers. One moment she was gone, the next she's risen through the rock. It comes in handy and yet Kit has never quite gotten used to it, even if she is the one who gets chastised for sneaking into places.

"Oh, Alma, we were wondering where you were," Kit says, even though that's not true.

"Why is nothing ever straightforward with you people?" Alma kneels and studies Nerissa with her marble-like eyes. She whistles lowly, but it is full of sand. "That doesn't look good. You're going to need someone who knows how to put snakes back together."

"I'm fine," Nerissa says, trying to raise her head. She hasn't yet taken issue with Kit's stroking and supporting.

"Not fine," says Worth. "You'll die if we're not careful."

"I have made some outstanding efforts in that respect," Nerissa says, rasping even more than usual, "and I believe I may be incapable of death..." There is something in her tone Kit doesn't like, a note of sadness. She is babbling, yes, but Kit doubts that Nerissa is lying.

"I'll go to the boat. Quickly. I can go very quickly," Kit says, gently extricating herself from Nerissa and almost falling back a step again once she regains her feet. Why is this happening? Since when is she anything other than fleet-footed? Her whole body feels as if it is cast in lead. "Someone should send word to Micheaux about Beti and whoever that was. And... Oph—Worth?"

"For now," says Worth.

"Can you stay with Nerissa?" Kit doesn't like where this is going. "It's only that I'm not sure what will happen..."

"If Ophaniel comes back?" Worth finishes her sentence. "I'm not sure, either. But while we don't see eye to eye on everything, we agreed to come here. And I can think of no better guardian for a wounded lamia than a creature of the heavens and a stout dwarf of Nith. We can't move her yet, anyway, I don't think."

"We'll send word to Dr. Plover," says Alma. "I know how to get a message to him. And he's the best in the business."

"Good," says Kit, nodding her head because it sounds like a good idea. But she doesn't know who Dr. Plover is.

Leaning down, Kit whispers in Nerissa's ear. "I'll be back before you know it."

She isn't sure if she imagines it, but Kit believes she sees a glimmer in Nerissa's eye reminiscent of affection before pulling away. Or it could just be the incandescent pain generally experienced during separation of one's body and their appendages.

8

ALWAYS A HITCH

The coast of Andalusia is rocky and brown when Christabel arrives, nothing near the vast, verdant hills she imagined. She supposes that's a silly notion, that Spain would be green, and yet she cannot help but be a bit disappointed in the barren rockiness.

The airport is small, the airplane even smaller, and she has a touch of green about the gills as she walks across the tarmac, squinting through her sunglasses in an attempt to find her contact, a long-time correspondent of Dr. Frye. Dr. Frye has remained behind in Scotland, which is just as well, but Christabel finds herself missing the batty witch. During their work together she complained many a time in her journals at night, but now that she's on her own her thoughts are too loud, and she could do with some of the doctor's constant babbling.

She does not expect to see Nerissa and Kit right away, of course; that would be absurd. They will be coming by boat, as they always do, and wouldn't be at an airport. Christabel does, however, silently curse herself when she looks for Worth's face in the crowd.

Ten years. Not long compared to the other immortals around her, but long enough for her to feel it. And nowhere not long enough to forget him; or, worse even, to give up hope altogether.

Her contact in the region is planning to pick her up by motorcar, so she was informed. She's had a long correspondence with this local supernatural individual—a term she prefers over "creature" or "monster" regardless of what Nerissa thinks—named Kalum Angelos. Judging by his archaic writing style and penmanship, she had him figured as an elderly, judgmental, scholarly fellow.

But the man leaning against the bright blue Wolseley Hornet does not suggest any of those descriptions. He is tall, lean, and effortless, with no hint of glamour about him. She has heard this is the case with many of the Greek-descended supernaturals, but she did not think he would be so...beautiful. His hair is the color of black walnut, his cheeks molded at precise angles to accentuate his full lips and curving smile. He wears dark glasses, wire-rimmed, and now she is looking at his hair again. It brings to mind a summer night, shod with just the most delicate wisps of silver.

"You've overdressed for the season," the man says. He looks at Christabel, not hungrily or lustily, but with a precision to which she is unaccustomed. He sees her. Deeply.

"Yes, well, I came straight from Scotland," she says. She does not falter, though her heart beats strong, and his voice makes her want to close her eyes and listen. "There are fewer climates more contrary than the Hebrides and the Andalusian coastline. I did not have time to make a stop for better clothing. And I presume you are Mr. Angelos?"

"Call me Kalum," he says, tipping his head forward as if he were wearing a hat. Which is he not, as coarse as it may seem. But Christabel is glad of it, because it would obscure that glorious hair. His English is accented with vowels of

Kent. She does recall him mentioning he studied at Canterbury.

"Kalum, then. I am Christabel Crane, as you have likely deduced. It is good to finally make your acquaintance," she says, holding out her hand.

Kalum takes her hand and turns it one way then another before shaking it gently. "You're so very American. And smaller than I thought you'd be."

"They always say such things about my sort. I suppose it's due to the general scarcity," she says. "Myths have a way of growing over the years."

"Your presence is immense in prose," he says.

"Well, I thought you'd be older."

"I am older," he says. "I just don't look it, I suppose."

"No, no, you don't."

"Thank you, I think." He lowers his voice, taking off his glasses for just a moment. His eyes are deep hazel green, amber in the middle, fringed with dark, glorious eyelashes. "You have the most complete glamour of any supernatural individual I've ever met. It's..." he replaces his glasses, "it's almost foolproof."

"Almost?" She hands him her luggage.

"It's in the eyes. The only place where the real you shines through. Like moonlight bursting through the clouds. Do you suppose you have two complete states?"

They both stand a moment, staring at each other. The wind whips Christabel's hair across her face, but she cannot find the strength to move it out of the way.

"If I do, it's one of the only recorded cases of it known to our history," she says, somewhat shyly. Studying herself is both a necessary and almost embarrassing line of work. "But as I have no one to compare myself to, it makes it rather difficult. Most supernatural individuals rely on glamours, glands, or telepathic ability to convince the onlooker that what they see is indeed human. And others, like yourself, appear human almost entirely."

"Ah, you don't know me yet to make that judgment," Kalum says with a laugh like honey, deep and rich.

Christabel presses at the bridge of her nose. The jet lag must be getting to her already. Such long travel does make her feel giddy, and Kalum is not helping matters at all.

Noting her state, Kalum gestures to the car. "Well, we best get going. Mother is waiting for us at the cottage, and she doesn't like to be left alone for long."

Mother? Ah, well. There's always something.

* * *

They drive southward down the coast toward a little town named Marbella. The quaint stucco houses and narrow roads break up the landscape, but Christabel can't help but almost enjoy herself. The sun is warm on her skin, the breeze a gentle counterpoint as she sits beside Kalum.

Yes, Kalum is very handsome. She steals furtive glances now and again, to make sure he really is at attractive as she recalls. The moment she looks away, she half forgets his face and must reassure herself that her memory was correct. So, she takes yet another look. Covert. Until he catches her and gives her a grin.

"I was surprised you came down where you did on the whole 'gods versus monsters' debacle," Kalum says casually. "Your correspondence on the matter was a bit spotty at the time, and I knew you were busy. But if it weren't for you, there might have been all-out war."

Ah, yes. *That.* While Nerissa and Kit kept Ophaniel, the angel that was once her boyfriend, in their London flat, Christabel worked closely with Dr. Frye not only on cataloguing the dwindling beast population but working as an emissary between gods—truly just monsters with natural human forms—and monsters for the better part of the last decade. It ended in court, a body she helped create with the help of the mostly reformed Circle of Iapetus, a human league dedicated to keeping the peace between monsters and humans.

"You know, I didn't think it would turn out so well, the Prague Accords," Christabel says. "You helped me quite a great deal with your research and notes. I never asked because I know it is impolite to do so, but I could tell you had considerable experience in similar circumstances."

"Gods and monsters have been fighting since the beginning of time," Kalum says, his voice softening, his gaze straying to the horizon. "Gods and their offspring are just lucky to pass in mixed company without raising eyebrows. Though it isn't that easy for us. I've been here in Marbella for the better part of the last two thousand years and I still feel like a stranger."

"Your name sounds local enough," she says.

Kalum laughs, shaking his head. "It's bastardized Latin, by way of Greece. Like Mother. Like Grandfather. Diluted, certainly, from the source. We're all a bit diminished these days. But certain... ah...circumstances still keep us here. Aside from my studies, I've not left Spain at all. So, I'm glad that the work I did was helpful. Precedence is necessary in these matters."

"It was very kind of you."

"Hardly. Your letters have always brought a challenge to my mind and a song to my heart. There are so few who are truly interested in the history of gods and monsters, to say nothing of the lesser beings."

"I always have been. Even when I was, as you say, 'passing' among the Circle of Iapetus. Though, twenty years ago they were hardly the league they are now."

"You're absolutely angelic to put up with them," Kalum says with another golden laugh. "I can't stand them."

"They grow on you after a while," she says with a chuckle. "Though finding you through Dr. Frye was a remarkable stroke of fate and certainly helped me bring the Circle, and myself, I suppose, to a position of more prominence. While Dr. Frye is primarily interested in the environmental ramifications of supernatural power, she grows tired of my questions. I know I'm young, but I like to think that it serves me well, my curious nature. So you were an essential conduit for my incessant lines of query."

"As I said, it was my pleasure. You've had the unique experience of living as a human for the first few years of your life," he says. "Most of us never have such a thing. My grandfather raised me for a time, and that was anything but typical. I had to work backward to connect to my humanity, and I'm still having to do that. So I valued your opinion and viewpoint. And look at you, the great peacemaker. Overall, relations between the god and monster factions have been good."

"I suppose I just feel as if I'm neither beast nor god," Christabel says softly. She wants to pour out her soul to Kalum, but she resists. Painfully. "I'm sorry, that doesn't make any sense; I'm exhausted."

"I think it makes sense if it's how you feel. I, however, would firmly categorize you as a goddess, given your glamour capabilities. You are entirely human most of the time, are you not?"

She nods slowly. "I seem only to shift when I'm...well, it's not very predictable, I should say. But yes. I am most comfortable when I am like this. It seems to be my natural state. And when I am in bestial form, it is not consistent. So perhaps that is why I relate better than my companions who have to work so hard to maintain their glamours to have even the barest of human experiences."

"Currently I teach at the University of Granada now and then. Classics, mostly, to ground myself in human experiences. It keeps me humble, I suppose. But I don't get out nearly as much as I should. I can never leave for long, not with Mother..." he trails off and brings the car to a stop.

They are at the foot of the mountains, now. There's a small winding path leading up and away to a square stone and stucco cottage, nestled so close to the hill it looks as if it's growing from the rock itself, like a strange square mineral. It is enclosed in so much rosemary that Christabel can smell it from the car, clean and bright and rich.

Christabel allows Kalum to open the door for her, and she has to shade her eyes from the bright light to see better. No sign of the aforementioned mother.

"You haven't spoken much about your mother before," Christabel says as diplomatically as possible. "I should have brought her a gift. I admit I feel a bit unprepared."

Kalum is looking back and forth between Christabel and the house. "You don't need to bring anything. She'll love to meet you. It's only that she's old. Very old. And she's often confused. And truly, one can never really prepare for Mother."

"You are a kind son to stay with her," Christabel says. There are many features she sees in Kalum, but kindness is not the first characteristic that comes to mind.

Kalum frowns slightly, then shakes his head. "For another time. For now, let us join and have some good wine. Do you drink? I hope you do."

* * *

Her name, Christabel quickly learns, is Makaria, and the wine is a comfort in the wake of her chaos. Makaria looks nothing like an old woman, and despite Kalum's protests to the contrary, she appears most ordinary, all things considered. Yes, she is about a foot taller than an average human woman. Yes, her hair is dark as pitch and light as smoke, and it forms a kind of moving art piece as she walks about, as if she is underwater. Yes, she dresses in black linen, and her arms are scarified rather intensely. But that is nothing compared to the kind of things Christabel has seen, having walked the Underworld more than once.

Makaria is so delighted at Christabel's arrival that she immediately pours three large glasses of dark purple wine and has a toast in her honor but forgets what she's doing halfway through.

"To a most magnificent creature," Makaria says. "To Christabel, who has come all the way from America to find... what is it you're looking for?"

"It's a bit of a missing person case," Christabel says. It is not the first time she has had to clarify. Makaria initially thought Christabel was asking to marry Kalum, which was momentarily confusing but not out of the realm of behavior for a woman of her means and bearing. "A sylph, to be precise. An unusual sylph."

"People go missing all the time, so I've learned, to say nothing of sylphs," Makaria says gravely. She's pouring more wine, and up until now Christabel has been very courteous about it, but she doesn't usually drink so much. It will not end well if she's not careful. Being drunk is not her preferred state.

"Mother, she doesn't mean it that way," Kalum says. "It's a friend of hers. And she's been missing for twenty years."

"Well, that's hardly a cause for concern," says Makaria. "I

once lost a husband for thirty years, and I barely missed him."

Christabel tries not to laugh because she's certain Makaria does not mean it in jest. Once she's composed herself, she clarifies, "Vivienne du Lac was abducted. By a djinni."

"Was she now?" Makaria is half-replying, and Christabel is painfully aware she's not getting very far.

"Yes, and it's—a bit—well, my fault. At least, I didn't help in the matter at all. I've solved dozens of cases in the last twenty years, helped forge alliances in the arcane community, read enough books to fill up this entire house, and all I had on Vivienne's whereabouts was dust. Until now. We have evidence she's been tied up in some rather underground groups."

"I like it underground," Makaria says wistfully.

Kalum sighs, shaking his head, and gives Christabel an apologetic look. "Not everyone does, Mother," he says. "And besides, that's not what Christabel means. She means that someone has taken her friend against her will, and no matter what they've done, they haven't found any indication of where she might be. But now they have, and it's brought them here."

Christabel notices a shift in Kalum's tone. Slight. But just enough. The word "here." It's not the way one would say, "Here, at home." It is more like, "Here, of all places." Which, it does not seem, is terribly welcome.

"Then she must not be looking hard enough," Makaria says to her flagon of wine. She sloshes it around, dips a finger in, and removes a fat cricket.

"But we've got reason to think that she may be in Andalusia," Christabel says. "Which I why I wrote Kalum in hopes that he could show me around a bit and see if there are any lingering clues."

Makaria frowns suddenly, her once rather confused and placid state evaporating before Christabel's eyes. "Oh, that won't do at all."

"Your pardon?" Christabel asks.

"Kalum, why do you bring such people to me? Why do you involve me so?" Makaria stands and throws her glass, wine and all, shattering into the fire. "As if you and I don't have enough business to attend. As if the family legacy can sustain another interloper."

Christabel has never felt so out of place in her life. She chokes back her protest, and puts down her glass of wine, sending her gaze to the door. Kalum catches her, though, and shakes his head. "Not yet" he mouths.

Kalum continues, his voice so gentle it's like silk across satin. "Hush, Mother. Please, we are not asking anything of you. No one wants to use you to their benefit. I promise. This is simply between Christabel and me."

"But what *is* she?" Makaria peers over. Her eyes are dark, judging.

"Just someone looking for answers," Christabel says.

"You stink of *celestials*." Makaria sighs, and this is not a benediction, nor is it acceptance. But she appears a little calmer now.

"I have a friend who is an angel, mostly," Christabel says. "Though the word friend is perhaps a little generous. It's been some time since I've seen them, though, so I can't imagine that's it."

She tells herself that she doesn't miss Ophaniel. That she's gotten over Worth. That she doesn't ache when she thinks about the way he used to look at her, the feeling of his fingers intertwined with hers...

She tells herself a lot of other lies, too.

"You aren't *using* it," Makaria says, holding up her hands as if to protect herself. "You aren't using it. You aren't."

"I didn't say I was," Kalum says. "I didn't ask to use it. We don't even have to talk about it, Mother. I just want to help Christabel."

Christabel wonders why she always falls for the broken, strange ones. Why couldn't she fall for a nice eunuch? Or a boring satyr? She is beginning to piece together Kalum and Makaria's demesnes. The way the darkness gathers about them, how the shadows leak from their eyes when she looks away and has them on the periphery. It does not frighten her; she's seen chthonics before, and they had giant scorpions on their heads. Considerably more frightening than some shadowy eyeliner.

Still, Christabel has the sense that Makaria has been betrayed before and Kalum is merely looking out for her.

"I'm sorry others have deceived you," Christabel tries lightly. "I mean no harm. I only want a local guide."

"Everyone wants the Pit of Hades," Makaria says, her tone punctuated, vicious. "How dare you claim you are free from its call. Haven't you heard it since the moment you set foot here? It calls *everyone*, child." She glances at her son, and then back to Christabel, knowing.

Christabel makes to stand, but Kalum holds up a hand, beckoning her to stay a moment longer. She can't say why, but she sighs and nods her assent. This is as close as she's managed to Vivienne in twenty years. And though she's a bit worried that she hasn't gotten word from Nerissa or Kit yet, she settles back, trying to pull her most innocent, charming, and lovely face.

"I will explain to her, Mother, if you'll permit me," Kalum says.

Makaria's eyes flicker back and forth between the others in the room, much longer than one might consider adequate for such judgment. Then she sighs and shakes her head, her long hair twisting about her in an invisible current.

"Very well," Makaria says. "But if she hurts us, I will call down vengeance."

"I have no doubt," Kalum says, warmly.

Then he turns to Christabel. "It all begins with my grandfather, a god named Hades…"

9

NO NATURAL-BORN MONSTER

Kissing Nadine was a bit strange at first, but now, most evenings, Vivienne has come to anticipate it. She can't remember exactly when it began, perhaps around their journey from Tunisia to Sicily when they ran into that tempest, but she isn't sure. All she knows is that being with Nadine, tasting her skin, is both physically warm—she embodies fire—and numb at the same time. And she is quite certain she would not be alive if she did not have such a connection to the ifrit.

Vivienne's chains prevent her from using her own power in such an endeavor, as she used to. A hundred years ago she would have risen up, taken the breath from a creature such as Nadine, and inhaled her, body and soul, fueling her desire, the passion a form of ethereal nourishment. It would be great pleasure for both of them, but even more for Vivienne. She used to feed on that power, sate her body with sex and lust and possession.

But now, not so. She must make do the way mortals must, and it isn't so terrible.

"Your skin," Nadine says, running her fingers across

Vivienne's belly, tracing the hollow of her stomach, trailing tongues of blue fire. Vivienne used to have a little rise there, a healthy glow, but now she is little more than a wraith. Still, the ifrit finds her beautiful. "It is like moonlight on snow. How is it so white without being transparent?"

"You forget that I'm a *monster*," Vivienne replies. Once she would have responded with power in her voice, that sturdy assuredness she once possessed. Now it is spoken softly.

"Tell me about how you were," Nadine says. "Please? Haven't I earned at least a glimpse by now?"

Vivienne reflects a moment inwardly and yes, were she to catalogue the indulgences in Nadine's favor, she would owe her a great deal on passion alone, to say nothing of friendship.

Until this moment, Vivienne has refused to answer the question. Trust came slowly between them, but then there it was, a full-fledged presence in their midst. And she is weary and a little drunk, and her lips are still warm from where Nadine kissed her moments before.

"I used to say that we monsters are all orphans, but that's not entirely true, is it?" Vivienne closes her eyes and tries to remember before she was Vivienne du Lac. Before she was *la belle dame sans merci*. Before she found her way to England, slinking through the fens like some hobbled creature. "I am no natural-born monster."

Nadine leans on her arm, tilting the angles of her face so beautifully that Vivienne smiles, resisting the urge to kiss her again. There is a childlike delight in Nadine, especially when Vivienne tells her tales. But until now she had not mentioned this life to anyone. Not even to Nerissa, at least not in full.

So she decides to tell a mostly truth.

"Oh, what a delight!" Nadine practically squeals with excitement.

"My mother was a nymph," Vivienne says. "And she was a sworn virgin of the Huntress, of Artemis."

At the name of the goddess, Vivienne swears she sees a flicker of surprise in Nadine's eyes. But the flame quenches as quickly as it came, and Vivienne's tongue is loosened with wine now. So much wine. Perhaps Nadine finds it ironic that Vivienne's mother was a virgin.

But Vivienne has enough presence of mind to obscure some of the facts. She cannot be entirely vulnerable. Even if all else is lost, she must keep some secrets, some power, to herself.

"My mother was named Aura. She was prideful, so they say. She dared compare herself to Artemis's beauty. Having overheard Artemis complain of Aura's treachery, Dionysus, who was in his usual drunken stupor and angry over a falling-out with Zeus, tracked Aura down," Vivienne explains. The story comes easier because it has been told so many times, just not by her. She feels the common line of the tale, the words forming before she even has time to consider them in full. "He saw Aura bathing in a stream, her long hair like a silver waterfall, and in his lust, he raped her, in hopes of claiming her beauty and possessing. I have read stories that claim Eros's arrow pierced his heart, or that Artemis put him up to it. But I do not believe it. What little my mother passed to me…"

Vivienne sits up and takes a long drink from the bottle of wine beside her, welcoming the hot sting of it on her lips. Her chains clink against the glass, and she sighs.

Nadine's fingers slip down Vivienne's pale back.

"They call the land Turkey, now, where I walked," Vivienne says. "But when I was a child, we called it Phrygia. My mother became pregnant by Dionysus and tried to drown the twins she birthed one night. In punishment for her crimes, she was turned into a fountain by Zeus, but not before her last labor pains."

Vivienne gestures to herself. "I had two brothers, and I do not remember them now, for they were raised among the new gods. I, born later, was given to my grandmother, Cybele, and raised deep within the mountain. They named me Apsinthos. Wormwood."

Nadine is silent, watching Vivienne's expression. "You remember all of this?"

"I was born with my mother's memories. They lived inside of me somehow, this dark fury and rage that I could not release," Vivienne says, holding up her fingers. "I was rebellious. Furious. I scorned my grandmother, I fled. My strange skin sought warmth but was never warm. I did not age. Men and gods fell before me and I became monstrous. I drank the blood of a thousand men, and I was still not satisfied."

"How ever did you stop?"

"I fell in love with a mortal," Vivienne replies, taking her once lustrous hair between her hands. "And I began to see the joy of humanity, as short-lived as it was. My beloved hated me in return, and though I knew I could woo him to my bed, I refused to use my power, and he left me. Desperate for love, I cried out to Artemis in the dark of night and heard only the whisper of the wind in the trees. I decided I would change myself. And I would seek out others like me who had been ill-made."

"I don't think you are ill-made," Nadine says, tracing Vivienne's cheek with her palm. "I think you are precisely what I was hoping."

"I am no goddess," Vivienne says.

"You are descended from goddesses. For isn't that what a nymph is? A child of Titans, or goddesses..."

"I have no desire to count myself as a goddess. Merely

one of their malformed progenies, wandering the earth for too long, and now chained."

Nadine frowns. "I wish we could be rid of these."

Vivienne is done talking about the lives she once led and is ready for another kind of escape. She draws the ifrit close for another kiss. As ever, Nadine does not resist. She is unquenchable, even under Vivienne's icy touch. Vivienne presses herself insistently over the length of Nadine's body, feeling every curve and variation in heat. Nadine's kisses are fire on her lips, filling her lungs with painful, lusty joy. Like breathing into a funeral pyre. Release and relinquish.

When Nadine's kisses reach her navel, Vivienne loses herself in the old dance, hips moving and hands clasping, tongue reaching and tasting. But she weeps, and her cries of joy mingle with those of sorrow.

* * *

Nadine falls asleep, and Vivienne does not. Her body grows cold as soon her lover leaves for the land of dreaming, and Vivienne shivers. She rises and goes to the high window above her bed, watching the moonlight shimmer across the pale stone walls, wishing she had the gift of sleep.

A little Spanish moon moth, the *Graesllsia isabellae*, flutters across the pane, waiting a moment on the edge of the window. Bereft of her powers, Vivienne sees the little creature differently than she might have before. Its lines are clearer, the small eyes on its wings stranger. The world is all hard angles and outlines, shifts in temperature and consistency and composition. But the moon moth is not afraid of her.

It alights on her hand, so gentle it almost tickles. The wings fold, and it rests quietly. Vivienne dares not breathe.

And she feels she should know this creature as if it is part of another, long-dead story where she once belonged. But her memories grow more sluggish the longer she is kept from her power.

Worth. Nerissa. Christabel. Aura.

Telling Aura's story was not been easy. She almost regrets it except she can't. She's had her guard up for so very long, so very, very long, that the expression of her former self feels a kind of release. She has lived so many lives over the thousands of years of her existence that she often forgets the details. Inevitably they return, though.

Another moon moth. Curious. Christabel would know the exact details, but Vivienne is fairly certain that they are on their way to extinction. She is about to reach out for the second when a third comes in through the window and lands on her shoulder, fair and light and luminescent.

The three moths then join in a circular gambol, twisting in and around one another, winding this way and that, until they start to flutter their way to the door behind her, leading out to the rest of the villa.

Vivienne stares at the barred door. It is not nearly as fortified as it has been during her incarceration; only so much to do in this old, remote villa. She may have dampened magic, but she can still be silent. The moths wait at the door, turning again and again, as she softly pads her way toward them.

Nadine is snoring. Her drinking is predictable; her sleep uninterrupted when it comes, which is not often. It would be best not to bother her.

As Vivienne runs her fingers over the lock, she is surprised to find how cold it is, as if she had been exerting her powers on it. Those long-lost powers once so easily possessed, to turn anything to ice, to draw heat from it and make frost. To feast on the warmth.

But it is not her magic. She breathes shallowly, casting a glance over her shoulder to see if Nadine still sleeps.

The moths twirl around her again and again, and Vivienne gently unlocks the door, the mechanism falling away under slight pressure. It makes her old heart, which pumps so much more slowly than a mortal's, quicken and rise to her throat. Is that joy she feels? Power? Hope?

The hallways are dark, and the tiles cool on her bare feet. Bastille's quarters are not far, but she cannot hear him or feel him at all. His presence is the only one she can attune to, some cruel fate of her incarceration. But helpful in a case like this.

Vivienne's moth companions flutter right and then left, then toward the cellars. *Come, come!* They seem to say. The entire house is utterly silent. No sign of Cygna. No sign of Bastille. She can smell the distant burn of petrol, hear the sighing of the sea in the distance.

But her moth friends do not lead her to freedom. No, they lead her elsewhere.

There are two entrances to the cellars: the one nearest her and the one via the kitchens. This one, by the living quarters, was likely intended to be the more impressive of the two, but a long-ago collapse has obscured the way and it is too much trouble to clear in such a short time. The moths linger there, patient, twirling.

But Vivienne is slight. Very slight. Even with her shackles, she is so silent, so tenuous, that one could almost mistake her for a shadow.

Ten steps down, however, and the stairway becomes treacherous. Gravel litters every step, the overhang so close to Vivienne's head she can touch it in places. Vines grow in, too. Honeysuckle and vetch, curling like the arms of an octopus down the wall. She does not want to look at them too long, for they seem to move, to threaten her, to spell out words.

She should have stayed in bed.

She almost turns around to find the comfort of Nadine's warm, drunk body, but then she catches the scent of an aroma so old and familiar she almost cries out in recognition. It is the thick, honey scent of asphodel.

Vivienne tries to rein in her excitement, mingled though it may be with much fear. A light glows dimly at the bottom, buttery yellow against the red clay walls. No one has seen her. No one will know. She must go just a little further.

She is about to reach the bottom step and turn to see what lies beyond, even though the hope in her breast tells her that she knows already, when a cold hand clasps around the back of her neck. Her shackles crackle in response, sending her to her knees.

A quick yank of her long hair and Vivienne is looking up into Bastille's face. Now that she is this close—or perhaps it is through the clarity of pain—she notes familiar lines. He is shockingly beautiful. Beautiful as the moon itself. But cold. So cold.

"Here, behold," Bastille says, grabbing Vivienne by the collar with tremendous strength. He flings the night sylph to one side, so she is staring at a small cell carved into the very earth. Vivienne knows the stone—of course she does—and she turns the thought in her head. Alabaster? Why alabaster?

There is a figure inside the cell. The source of the asphodel scent. She is somehow half-sunken into the stones; they crawl up her body like lichen.

"You see? My gift to my lady Cygna. Bowed and bent and in her rightful place," Bastille says.

"Artemis," whispers Vivienne.

Artemis is just as tremendous as Vivienne remembers, a

massive woman of corded muscle and power. Her square face is punctuated by thick lips and dark-lashed eyes, eyes as white as alabaster themselves. She was never a wispy beauty, but one of earthy power and absolute presence. Even now, trapped as she is, Vivienne feels that power, diminishing though it may be. Artemis nods slowly, Bastille barking a laugh.

"I didn't expect to see you here, Aura," Artemis says.

10

NITWITS

Ophaniel comes back to himself, and there is a wounded snake woman at his feet bleeding all over the place. He vaguely remembers coming here, deciding at last that staying in his tower forever might not be the best course of action—and because of Worth's incessant pushing—but now he's quite confused as to where he's been the last bit of time.

Sorry about that, old chap. Didn't meant to take the helm. But you weren't doing much to help, and I was afraid we weren't going to make it.

"We were attacked," Ophaniel says out loud, forgetting that the snake woman can hear.

"Of course, we were attacked, you nitwit," Nerissa growls. "Do you think I just chewed off my arms because I was hungry? Now give me a piece of cloth and help me bandage this."

She is breathing in and out very fast, and Ophaniel first wonders why she doesn't grow another limb, then realizes, of course, that she is not a celestial, and while she is supernatural, she cannot regenerate so easily.

Ophaniel has little in the way of clothing, but long strips of linen wrap his legs, more out of propriety than a sense of fashion. He has tried walking around naked, his preferred state, but has not been able to do so in his present company. So he is more than glad to oblige.

The creature's blood is green, but it dries blue on his hand. Ophaniel is not familiar with bodies that ooze and seep and so he has to look away numerous times.

"Angels don't bleed," he says. It doesn't sound apologetic the way he says it, but he means it as such. "We can be redistributed, but we cannot die from loss of blood or organs. We are creatures of pure energy, so we require no such barbaric structures beneath our skin."

"Aren't you just the luckiest?" Nerissa's form is unchanged, her glamour flickering through her pain. Ophaniel has not had occasion to look at her that way, and he finds she is not as strange as he imagined. Well, no, that isn't right. She is hideous, but there is a rhyme and reason to her form. Her mottled skin and yellow eyes, the long waves of her hair, the scales at her cheeks and neck. He can at least recognize that she is well-made, even if she is a horror to gaze upon. Even if the two bloody stumps at her side make him feel as if he is looking into the very Void itself.

"I thought we had a boat to catch," Ophaniel says, trying— hoping—to make pleasant conversation.

Nerissa closes her eyes tight, her jaw clenching. "Ophaniel, could you oblige me with silence while I writhe in pain? I may be no angel, but I have some capacity for healing. Though…" She grunts, agony seizing her features again for a moment. "If you do not keep quiet with your angel prattling, I may let myself die just to avoid having to listen to you any longer."

Ophaniel realizes that this is a jest, but it doesn't make

him laugh. He doesn't understand Nerissa's humor. There is nothing prattling about him.

He's just lonely.

Or would be, if Worth would leave him alone.

Let her have some air. Keep an eye out for that dwarf.

Nerissa leans back and then reaches into her satchel to retrieve the disgusting imp ichor she's become increasingly dependent upon. If he cared about her, he'd tell her that it wasn't healthy for her, that there were better options, or at least less-addictive ones, and that she shouldn't listen to vampires. Look where she ended up!

But he doesn't say anything.

Once she has a drink of the stuff, her lids get heavy a moment and then, with a barely perceptible shimmer, she slides back into her mostly human guise, minus the arm. There's only so much one can do with magic, after all.

Rather than say anything inappropriate, Ophaniel just goes motionless and waits, listening.

"Was I imagining things, or was Worth talking through you earlier?" Nerissa's voice is a little less strained now.

Ophaniel doesn't like the question. He doesn't quite know the answer, himself, but he's aware that Nerissa is fond of Worth and, in the measure of non-angels, it must have been a traumatic experience.

"It's possible," Ophaniel says.

Nerissa gives him a strange, measuring look. Her eyes are still yellow. So the glamour isn't *that* strong. "How long has he been chattering in your head?"

Ophaniel just stares at her. He thinks he's very coy and clever about the whole thing, but the conversation quickly disintegrates.

"You've been talking with him this whole time," Nerissa says, struggling to get to her feet. She's wobbly. And if it weren't for the fact that Ophaniel felt the dwarf person returning, he would grab Nerissa to steady her. "For ten years you've been talking with him and you failed to make mention."

"I don't much like you," Ophaniel says in his candid way. "I didn't think it was an important detail."

Ophaniel is afraid of her for just the barest of seconds, given the look of poisonous fury in her eyes. But the dwarf shows up first. And on deeper consideration, Ophaniel thinks that Alma makes a much better recliner for a woozy lamia than he does. Touching her skin makes him want to retch, and he doesn't want to talk about Worth, because admitting it makes it real. And angels aren't supposed to have competing personalities.

"If I had all my appendages I would strangle you with all of them right now," Nerissa says between gritted teeth.

"Whoa, now, whoa," Alma says, reaching up to take Nerissa around the waist.

"Where's Kit?" Nerissa asks, gathering her breath.

"You were supposed to *help* her," Alma says, accusingly, to Ophaniel. "Not deposit her like a sack of oats."

The angel shrugs. "I don't bleed. Angels heal by singing. But cherubim songs would make her eyes explode, to say nothing of the long-term hearing damage. What do you expect of me?"

This, finally, stops the lamia from her excessive whining and whimpering, while the dwarf tends to her. Ophaniel enjoys the quiet of the cave, and he wonders about its provenance. London isn't particularly old by the measure of angels. But it's old enough that he can't remember its precise beginning or end. There were humans here a very long time ago, and of course, since there were humans, there were also monsters. And gods and angels and all manner of creatures in between.

Nerissa feels familiar to the place, though, in a way that

Kit certainly doesn't. He doesn't remember Vivienne, this once paramour of Worth's, but he has a sense that she doesn't fit in quite so well. Nerissa is not a saltwater creature; she is an earthy creature, reminiscent of deep wells and cold springs in the mountains.

"Can you please stop staring," Nerissa finally says. She has shrugged off most of the pain, it seems, and is now walking around in a circle, more or less humanoid to the naked eye.

"I was just wondering about your provenance," Ophaniel says.

They walk a few steps toward the shoreline, the eerie moonlight casting glittering streaks across the water.

"My what?"

"Provenance," Ophaniel says. "I mean—"

"I know what you mean," Nerissa replies. "But I'm not a piece of furniture. I don't have *provenance*."

Ophaniel knows she's not a piece of furniture. But to an angel, the differences between furniture and non-angelic beings is very subtle. Armchair. Lamia. Divan. Sylph. Ottoman. Dwarf.

Subtle.

"Very well, then," he assents. "Your place of origin, to be more specific. Every monster has a beginning."

"I'm from here, of course," Nerissa says as if it's the most obvious thing in the world.

"I surmised as much," Ophaniel replies. "But specifically. This region?"

"Nearly, yes," Nerissa's teeth clatter together. She's cold. At least colder than she should be.

"Malham Tarn is the first place I remember," Nerissa says, half to the water. "The fens there, they're alkaline. Vivienne… when she found me, she said she thought that was one of the reasons I was so vicious, so wild. Something in the composition reacted badly with my already difficult tendencies."

Alma is looking sideways at the lamia, though. "I don't know. You have some features that I would consider consistent with this area, but I sense you're from a little further afield."

"What do you mean?" Nerissa's voice takes on a sharp tinge. Irritation.

"Only that I am an expert in soil. And minerals. And we creatures, or monsters, are imbued with imprints from where we were made. You remind me of...well, the Mediterranean. Or deeper?"

"Deeper? That's not a location."

"I could take a sample and find out," Alma offers.

For some reason, Nerissa finds this extremely offensive, judging by the size of her eyes in response. But thankfully, there is no time to resort to fisticuffs or anything, because Kit returns.

The furry one—she is not furry right now, but on occasion sprouts any number of tails and ears—is breathing hard and not smiling, and Ophaniel has learned from experience that this likely indicates she is upset. Given the last half hour's events, this seems an expected reaction.

"The boat...is on...fire," Kit says between breaths. And indeed, she smells like smoke, and there are smudges on her face. "Someone knew we were coming."

"So I lost two arms for nothing?" Nerissa is joking. Perhaps. She looks like she might faint, and Ophaniel does not think that's a good thing. Even though he would appreciate the quiet.

"Fire doesn't bother me," Ophaniel suggests, more to get out of this awkward situation with his companions. Nerissa has been kind to him, he understands this, but she also grates on him. And he feels uncomfortable when the furry one looks at the lamia too long, and vice versa. "I can go look."

Flying is complicated but running is not. And since

cherubim aren't tied to time in the same way most creatures are, Ophaniel can blink forward toward the right destination so long as he can see the next location. It's a trick of light, and not complicated, but challenging to teach to those convinced that their mortal bodies are so inflexible.

That isn't quite right. He forgets. Someone told him once that even immortal non-celestials would turn into pasta should they travel by such means. There was a specific pasta. Rigatoni? No, cavatappi.

There is a chance that the others would try and prevent him from going, but he is already too far away to hear their startled cries.

* * *

The boat is easy to find because it is indeed a great conflagration. It's been a long time since Ophaniel has seen such a display, and for a moment he considers just watching it. He's always liked the way that flames rise and fall, how the colors indicate the temperature and the fuel, how the smells and the sounds become so intermingled.

It appears as if some of the local mortals have given up on trying to save the boat. There is enough smoke that most of them are doubled over, coughing into their sleeves, or just sitting on metal buckets and shaking their heads.

If Vivienne were here, it would be fairly obvious.

Worth is there again, and Ophaniel bats at him internally. But that never works.

"Why won't you go away?"

Trust me; I would if I could. I'm starting to think I've always been part of you. I would like rest, but it appears I won't get it. I can help you in this instance. As I said, Vivienne always leaves an impression. She is, by nature, incredibly cold. She is also a restless soul who can never keep her hands still. She would have left her handiwork somewhere.

"It's burning too fast."

No, it isn't. Not for you. For us. It looks like they started the fire in the forecastle. But I doubt anyone would have kept Vivienne that far away, knowing her capabilities. A sylph on a ship would require an enormous amount of power to contain, what with the presence of water everywhere. They would have wanted her nearby.

"You don't make much sense."

I never claimed to. But I do feel a bit cheated about the fireproof bit. When I was in control, I could have been a rather dashing fellow when it came to rushing into dangerous situations. This whole time I could have simply walked through the fire.

Ophaniel doesn't know what to say about the whole walking into a burning boat business. There is so much about being a celestial that he has forgotten. He hoped it wouldn't take long to return, but so long as Worth is around, Ophaniel is never quite right. Never quite back to himself.

He doesn't remember being able to walk into flames. And they look rather terrifying.

I can do it if you don't want to.

But when Ophaniel goes to answer, it isn't as if he has a choice.

11

ANGELS ON A PINHEAD

L iving inside of an angel for ten years has taken a toll on Worth Goodwin, a condition made no easier by having always been this angel and living a few hundred years of his life blissfully unaware. Thinking he was a Questing Beast—the Glatisant—he enjoyed a relatively acceptable life as a monster, and monster hunter when the world needed it. He fell in love a few times. He enjoyed newspapers. He preferred Bach over Beethoven.

But now he is an echo inside of his true self. Taking over Ophaniel's body is almost impossible when he's in hiding, up there in his apartment overlooking the misery of Shoreditch (and what kind of name is that, anyway?). But out here, in the danger and the heat, Worth is capable of much more. While he has not been the dominant portion of the celestial these ten years, he has been able to do something Ophaniel has not: he has observed. He has walked around the chambers of the angel's heart. He has taken stock. He has been quiet when Ophaniel hoped he was gone.

Worth sometimes wonders if his life has ever been anything but this.

But he remembers a face, one he has not seen in a very long time. And, like a beacon, it guides him forward.

Christabel.

To the task at hand, however. There is a burning ship before him, and there may be remnants of his once paramour, Vivienne du Lac, there. Unlike Ophaniel, Worth understands the sylph better than even she does. He can smell her in the burning fire, see her footsteps in the curls of smoke. She is not here, but she was before. Though judging by the state of things, it's been some time since she was aboard. It must have returned after taking her to Andalusia, if that's where she truly is.

Worth wonders if he's ever sensed Vivienne like this before or if it's just an added benefit of his being an angel now. Or part of one. He hasn't decided if he's merely a figment of Ophaniel or a legitimate secondary personality. Or, and this is the one he thinks about more often, neither of them is particularly the right being. Worth and Ophaniel are just echoes of someone else.

True to his suspicion, he is undeterred by the flames. It doesn't stop him from reflexively holding up his arms—he once had a body that he presumes was flammable—but all he feels is a light tickling along his forearms. Heat, yes, but it is only bothersome around the tenderest of his skin: his eyes, his lips, the spaces between his toes.

Bursting through the captain's quarters, he wishes someone were there to observe his heroics.

Alas, time is of the essence; as the fire rolls over the ceiling above him like a thousand yellow tongues, he grabs everything he can: Manifests, charred maps, a pile of pens, a small radio. Whoever left the boat to burn did not care to clean up after themselves, and while that is on the one hand rather thrilling—he does love some good evidence—Worth is smart enough these days to know the makings of a potential trap.

They have been seeking Vivienne's captor for twenty years. They were brought here with an anonymous tip. Or at least, a tip from a vampire, which is even worse than anonymous. And what's left of their vampire tour guide is currently a pile of skins on the shore behind him. This whole business reeks.

He has no pockets and immediately realizes that walking around naked clothed in nothing but glory has significant drawbacks. So Worth must simply grab as much as he can before the boat gives way and crumbles beneath him.

Just as Worth is about to depart, the edges of Ophaniel brightening his vision, he spots the curve of a familiar cheek laid upon the writing desk now slipping into fiery oblivion. It is in the form of a sketchbook. Each page flips with the fury of fire, but one drawing is unmistakable. Her face is as perfect as ten thousand marble statues; her neck is long and lean, her shoulders bare and draped and her bones…and on the next page, lace, just a small roundel slipped between the burning pages. Charred though it may be, there is no doubt whose hands crafted the delicate design.

* * *

"You really are in there, aren't you?"

They are now inside a cab, one of the underground sort available to them due to Christabel's connections with the Circle of Iapetus. It may be the one useful thing about the Circle. The cab has dark windows and is helmed by a grindylow named Greg.

Nerissa is looking straight across at Worth, as Ophaniel has not yet returned from his brooding depths, into his eyes. Alma has done an excellent job patching her up, but it is unlikely the lamia will heal. And she isn't exactly keeping consciousness consistently.

"It is me," Worth says. "For now."

Kit is there, staring at him measuredly from beneath her curtain of black hair. She has become very possessive of Nerissa, and Worth doesn't think that's a bad thing. If only Nerissa could see what esteem she's got right in front of her.

"We need to talk about the bleaknesses," says Kit, tapping her foot. "And we can't stay here too long, you know. There is a fire out there. And people will be looking for the hands that made the fire. And although we know we didn't do it, we've still got a celestial covered in smoke stains."

"They're tough to get out of feathers," Worth says, reaching back to pull at the useless wings behind him. "And I couldn't figure out how to blink on my way back. I'm sorry it took so long."

"She needs medical attention," says Alma. "More than I can give her. I'm not an expert on globulin-rich creatures. It's just a green mess. Her blood has oxidized copper in it, and it makes me sneeze."

"We have to find Vivienne," Nerissa says. "Forget about me."

"Always the stubborn one," Worth says.

"Hell, I've missed you, Worth." The lamia's eyes are tearing up. Worth watches in utter shock. Though he's seen her through Ophaniel's eyes almost every day for the last ten years, he's never seen her facade so broken. It must be the pain.

Kit gives Worth a very pointed look. It isn't at all subtle and involves waving of her hands and the universal sign for "death and dying" which is a slitting motion across the neck, followed by wild gesturing at Nerissa. He almost laughs. But she is right.

"Nerissa Waldemar," Worth says. "You stubborn monster.

We're going to have to pick up this thread when you've stopped bleeding, and we can get you someone better suited."

Nerissa rolls her eyes like a petulant child, but her lids flutter, too. She won't be lucid for long, and at least at that point, they can pull her away bodily. "Very well. But for the record, I was against meeting him again."

* * *

By "him" Nerissa means a man named Dr. Plover. Worth was briefly a clerk to Dr. Plover ages ago when he and Nerissa lived in London, during the height of their business, long before she and Vivienne escaped to America to avoid him (the story is perhaps more complicated than that but Worth likes to stick to the simpler version). Nerissa has never liked him because she doesn't like nice things. And Dr. Plover is very nice.

Dr. Plover is also a bird. And this bothers Nerissa, Worth suspects, because deep down she hates her own form and thinks that all monsters and beasts should have a proper guise even when interacting among themselves. Though Dr. Plover claims he cannot produce a convincing glamour, Nerissa has always believed he simply does it to be different, and such behavior has always bothered her. Worth sees through this facade, however, and understands that she is just jealous of Dr. Plover as he lives his life without regret and hiding, and that is a price above rubies.

Kit will not leave Nerissa's side, so Worth suggests that Alma be the one to send a message to Christabel, who will be expecting them in Andalusia. The charred remains of the ship manifest confirmed their suspicions: the crew was dropped not far from Gibraltar.

But Alma is the best choice, not simply because she's less emotionally involved with the whole Vivienne business, but also because she's capable of traveling through stone and has remarkable skills tracking down creatures aboveground. Alma has had to give up much of her status among dwarves to work with their motley crew, but Worth suspects she is glad of the distraction. From what he has gathered, family politics among the dwarves are even worse than among angels.

"Worth…" Kit is looking at him with a shocked face. "You're… you."

Worth looks down at his hands and can see that, indeed, he is wearing a glamour very much like the last one he wore for centuries. He wasn't planning on that. He finds himself rather emotional, having been attached to that face, those hands, that pocket watch.

I gather you can't walk around naked.

Ophaniel.

How astute of you. You're helping me, now? I thought you wanted to be rid of me.

I don't know what to do with you. Or with me. I don't like walking through fire. I don't like watching creatures bleed. I shouldn't have left my roost.

Ophaniel has always called the rooftop apartment his roost, and it amuses Worth to hear him use the phrase again.

"Ah, Worth?"

It is perilously tricky to have two conversations at once, especially when one of them is playing out inside your head.

"I cannot account for it right now," Worth says, and it's true.

Nerissa is losing a great deal of blood.

"Greg, my good man," Worth continues to the cabby. "Please telephone the Circle when you can and have an inquest begun into the London coven. If you can find Micheaux, please do. I am not sure how far the infection went, but I suspect it was just these two. Still, he is at risk."

"Of course, sir," says the grindylow.

"And wire Dr. Frye, if you're able to locate her."

"Done, sir."

"Excellent. Thank you, Greg." Worth takes a deep breath. It's a relief and a bit frightening to be back to his old self.

They all look at him, expectantly, so he says, "Kit, please ring the bell."

The bell is in the form of a feather dangling from the middle of a heart and is located halfway down the huge green door. They are in Notting Hill, which is as posh a place as can be, and yet entirely befitting Dr. Plover. Thankfully, the entrance to his office is charmed, and they are in no real danger of being seen. Hopefully.

Someone is watching, still.

This is another strain Ophaniel's been on lately. But he's always on some paranoid delusion or another. It's the celestial sight, he calls it.

We are fine. Stop being such a bother.

Don't say I didn't warn you.

12

BLOOD OF THE OLD WORLD

W orth, or Ophaniel, or whoever the angel is now, tried to prepare Kit for this Dr. Plover, but she didn't anticipate that the bird would be wearing human clothing. When they open the door, the white bird flies to a ready-made perch roughly the size of an average humanoid. This close, Kit can see the impeccable details about the creature: all the patterns on his tiny suit— arabesque if she's not mistaken—are done in miniature, all the way down to a tiny pocket watch chain coming out of a tiny pocket.

"That is the smallest pocket watch I have ever seen," Kit says, leaning forward and forgetting all appropriate decorum. "And I have seen many pocket watches. I briefly collected them."

"My proportions are somewhat smaller than the average clockmaker might be used to," says Dr. Plover, tilting his head to the side with a gauging glance from his bead black eyes. "But it is functional, I assure you."

The bird, an actual plover, has a white and black pattern across what plumage is visible, so it looks as if he's wearing a little wig. Kit finds him incredibly amusing but knows that she's already been impolite. It's ever difficult to keep her mouth shut in such situations.

Nerissa moans an incoherent phrase about a donkey. Even in the short ride over, she has slipped further away into a place of pain. And the exertion of going up the stairs about did her in.

"All the bantering aside," Worth says. "We have a situation."

Dr. Plover raises his beak, then nods. "The lamia, I see. Bring her into the parlor, and we will begin the examination."

Kit is curious as to how a parlor would be a proper place for a dying lamia—the thought bringing her up short for a moment—but she sees as soon as they get Nerissa through the door that the house is scoured clean save for the entrance. The entirety of the place is either painted white or else tiled brilliantly, and it smells of lavender and antiseptic. The walls that are not whitewashed are lined with shelves upon shelves of items, medical and arcane, all arranged by color across the spectrum.

As she stares as the ochres turning to chartreuse, Kit thinks that this is a kind of art. Not just a healing art, but a visual one as well. She has never seen such an arrangement of scientific items, and it strikes her as a curious contrast to the dark, shattering world around them. For isn't that what's happening?

The bleaknesses. Kit shudders as she helps arrange the lamia on a long metal table in the middle of the parlor, pushing aside the monsters in her memory. Two serving women dressed in nurse's garb come from either side of the room with thick linens, salves, and more modern transfusion devices.

"Annie, fetch me the calcium citrate, if you would," says

Dr. Plover, now positioned at another perch, just to the top of Nerissa's head.

Kit notices the further deterioration of her friend. Each scale, once iridescent forest green and gray, is now limned with a touch of orange, like a flower dying at the edges. It makes Kit feel ill to look upon her, as if she is seeing a true marvel of the world falling apart in her hands.

And isn't that what she is seeing?

"Lamias have difficulty processing certain chemicals," Dr. Plover explains. "Common in their species. The calcium citrate works wonders to clot. But that is the least of our problems. Lamias are unique in their blood systems, common in old-world nymphs of her sort."

"Her blood is copper-based," Kit says softly, leaning over to touch the side of Nerissa's face but stopping short. She catches Worth's eye and looks away.

Dr. Plover's ruff fluffs a bit. "Yes, that's correct. She needs oxygen, of course, like most creatures. But in her case, it's hemocyanin that carries the oxygen throughout her body, and it's comprised of two copper atoms and an oxygen atom."

Until this moment, Kit had never considered what her blood is made of at all. She has always assumed it was just blood. But Nerissa always says that she smelled of violets. Perhaps her blood is full of flowers.

"I see," says Kit.

The nurses work quickly to remove what clothing Nerissa has left on her body, gently moving the hair off her shoulders and plaiting it to keep it out of the way. The glamour slipped off somewhere between transit and arrival, but Kit honestly can't remember when.

She's starting to worry. She keeps looking at the stubs at Nerissa's side, hearing the lamia's pained cries, and wondering to herself why she's never been forward with her. Never thanked her. Never said what she felt.

Kit has never been in love before. Or at least, it's been so long that she can't remember. And how should a fox love a lizard? It's as improbable as the moon and sun loving one another. And yet...

"Kit, hold my hand," says Nerissa. It's soft, but Kit hears it and runs to her side to slip her small fingers into Nerissa's long, strong ones. Nerissa's grip is far weaker than it should be, but Kit tries to pour all her strength into assuring her.

"We fought creatures that we think are..." Worth struggles, and it's clear to Kit now that he's fighting off Ophaniel, or exhaustion, or both. He trembles, sweating, brushing his hands through his hair. "We think..."

"Worth, I am quite capable of managing this now that we are with Dr. Plover," Kit says, her voice rising above the din. "I recommend that you see to our other associate and return when you have rested."

Worth nods slowly. "I'm sorry, Dr. Plover...but it's been quite a day. I would try and explain to you exactly what happened, but I fear it currently defies even my understanding."

The bird shakes his head. "No apologies from you, Mr. Goodwin. I always knew you were beyond my realm of understanding, and I am glad that I was not mistaken in my conjecture. But yes, the *kitsune* is correct. Please attend to what you need. I am more than capable of helping Ms. Waldemar, providing I get enough information and we can work quickly. You should go to the kitchen and get something to drink; coffee, perhaps."

Worth's eyes brim suddenly with tears.

"Please, Worth," Kit says. "I can do this. I promise. I need to do this."

Worth retreats toward the kitchen, and Kit is glad of it. There is enough torture between them already that having another conflicted soul in the room feels almost too much to manage.

"The creatures. Tell me about them," Dr. Plover says once Worth is gone and the nurses have prepped Nerissa.

The nurses give the lamia a shot from a vial filled with a creamy white fluid, and Nerissa immediately goes slack. Kit feels both relief and worry wash over her in turns.

"Miss?"

"My name is Kamiyama Kumi. I am three hundred years old." She doesn't know why she says that, but it feels essential. There were many times she wanted to tell Nerissa that, and yet, she had always just been "Kit." And that was enough. But no, it wasn't. She should have told her more.

Dr. Plover nods his head. "Then tell me, Miss Kamiyama. Where are the lamia's arms? Because according to my preliminary examination, while they are not on her person, they are living—and in pain—somewhere else. Which I think is the reason for her current state and deterioration."

The realization of Nerissa's state is shocking to Kit, and she has to hold herself upright by balancing on a small stool. She perches when she's stressed, a habit Nerissa usually finds irritating, but Kit honestly doesn't know how else to deal with such emotions. It comes as natural to her as breathing. Perhaps it's a defense mechanism; that was Christabel's theory, anyway.

Either way, Dr. Plover does not point out that Kit is perching on a stool like a bird, nor that she is letting her tails show. Unlike Nerissa's glamour, which takes constant effort to maintain, Kit's physical forms ebb and flow, as simple as changing facial expressions. But there is no doubt that when she is emotional, she errs toward the fox.

"We fought creatures," Kit says softly. "I cannot describe them to you other than to say that they were not made of matter the way you and I are. And I do not simply mean made of feather or fur. They behaved badly, and at first, took the expression of two vampires we somewhat knew. I have little care for vampires myself, but that has more to do with their general lack of hygiene when it comes to their feet. Did you know that vampires have the ghastliest toenails?"

Dr. Plover lets out a short chirp and then settles on the taller nurse's shoulder. "I do, in fact, Miss Kamiyama. I am sadly, perilously, acquainted with the shortcomings of vampire podiatry. I have been working with the population for years, hoping to help them in this matter, but that is neither here nor there. I cannot say what it is that your friend has fought, but it appears that she is…"

Nerissa moans, and it ends in a whimper. Kit has never heard the lamia sound so small and helpless.

"The body is confused," Dr. Plover says. "Whatever these creatures—what did you call them?"

"I call them 'bleaknesses' because that's the best word I can think of in English. It's a slippery, rubbery language, English. But occasionally I find a decent enough word." Kit sighs, shivering and pulling her knees in even tighter. She likes the feeling when her hair trails down the front of her shins, and she does this for a moment, watching as the nurses and Dr. Plover attend to Nerissa. "It reminds me of an old story."

"Go on," says Dr. Plover.

"You probably think me quaint," Kit replies. "You're trying to save Nerissa's life, and I did nothing to stop the bleaknesses, and now all I can relay to you are stories."

Dr. Plover stops his commands to the nurses—"take the pulse there, no there, you know the lamias don't have the femoral artery placement," or "she is losing blood and if you don't keep pressure on that stump we're going to be in real trouble," or "double-check her other wounds; there may have been something that we missed"—and looks Kit squarely in the face.

His little black eyes are so piercing, so full of wisdom, knowledge, and sadness, that Kit almost feels embarrassed before he speaks.

"We live in a world of gods and monsters, Miss Kamiyama," Dr. Plover says. "And though you are many centuries younger than I, and inexperienced in some ways of this wild world, I can tell you with utmost conviction: stories are just as powerful as any force in heaven or on earth. What moves our hearts, moves our minds. What moves our minds, moves our hands. You and I, Nerissa and Worth, we are all tied together by forces no one truly understands. If something moved in you, please, I beseech you, tell me."

Kit has never heard anyone speak like this before. She feels at once proud of who she is but also stricken with a deep desire to be home, to be in Japan, to climb the mountains of her childhood and eat wild berries in the hillsides.

"When I was a child, they told me a story of the Dread Star," she says, though she calls him by his true name, *Ama-tsu-mika-boshi*. "He was a powerful god, but so far away. My mother told me he was out in the heavens, awaiting revenge from his fall. But that his evil was not evil the way we were taught. It was an evil of nothing. Not the good emptiness that comes of meditation and prayer and fasting, the emptiness that is a sky hunger."

"And there we are, little one; you are moved to the truth, though you know not the facts," Dr. Plover says, and Kit does not argue. Though he is a small creature in current stature, he is much larger than she. But only that his heart has more capacity, she thinks. "I have not shared news with you because I was not sure whom to trust. I have written to Dr. Frye, I have written to the Shah, written to Yer Iyesi. It is not the first outbreak of these bleaknesses, as you call them, but it is the worst."

"What is the cause, then?" Kit is afraid to ask, but does so anyway.

Dr. Plover sighs, hiding his head behind his wing for a moment, the tiny pocket watch clinking inside his vest. "Someone has kidnapped a goddess. A powerful, old goddess. Diana. Artemis. Potnia Theron. She has gone missing, and in her place, these bleaknesses have appeared—if that is what one could call it. And she is not the only supernatural creature to go missing over the last few decades, as I think you are well aware."

"We were headed to Spain," says Kit, slowly putting the pieces together. "To find Vivienne. We'd been searching for years. Then suddenly, we had a lead. But on our way, we were attacked. Nerissa was suspicious that the pieces were falling into place too easily. You don't suspect we're being lured?"

"Lured to kill. You did mostly survive an assassination," says the plover. "But only just. Yet I wonder, would they have let you live? All the clues were laid out for you, it seems."

"Why? I don't understand."

"One must never try to reason with madness," Dr. Plover says sadly, "but accept its repercussions and work to mend them."

"Nerissa will stop at nothing to find Vivienne," Kit says. "She will want us to go to Andalusia, even if she suspects death may follow us."

"I can help, however small. But listen to me: We are going to have to sever Nerissa's body from her missing limb, as I believe it will act as a beacon to you. For now, being hidden from these beasts of nothingness is your only chance. If we do not sever her connection from the missing limb, they will find her. They will find you. They will find London. And we will be part of the bleakness forever. But we will have to capture her, mostly, in her glamour, for it to work."

13

OLYMPIANS EN MASSE

I t always goes back to Hades, Christabel thinks. It isn't that she dislikes his stories; it's that she has grown tired over the years of the Greek pantheon and its trouble. Human beings find them inspiring, amusing, even naming buildings and cities after them. But the more Christabel has studied them, the more she has come to believe that they were really the worst of the divine. Monsters, even. Or more deserving of the name. And she knows this personally, having somewhat unintentionally fallen into a relationship with one of them a while ago.

As Kalum speaks of his grandfather, Christabel finds herself wishing she could have a word with the old rascal.

And that wouldn't be so difficult, as she learns, because according to Kalum, his mother Makaria guards the literal portal to the underworld, a one-way gate to Hades himself, kept safe by generations of their family.

"More properly, *one* of the underworlds," Kalum corrects. They have been talking for over an hour, and Christabel is beginning to wonder how she ever let herself slip into delusions of romance about this man. She must be tired, indeed.

"Hades is not as all-powerful as some think, he's merely gotten the bulk of the Western narrative. You know how it goes."

Christabel doesn't exactly, but she nods anyway. Yes, Hermes would agree with that, she thinks, trying very hard not to think about her disastrous romantic fling with the god. She didn't know it was him at the time of course, and well…his eyes were so very alluring.

Makaria is making another dinner, despite the fact Christabel insisted she'd had enough food to eat and indeed, she must be on her way. But the woman is having none of it.

Kalum steeples his fingers like a learned professor. "Of course, there shouldn't be portals to the underworld—this or any other—simply open to the general public. It's a danger to every and any creature coming within arm's distance. Present company excluded, of course. And, perhaps that's why your friend's captors took up residence nearby. Though, it's really mortals we must worry about because they are inexplicably drawn toward it. They can't help it. We routinely have to sweep the grounds for wanderers."

He says it almost lovingly.

"And can no one else take turns with you?" Christabel asks. She has decided that being part of the conversation is less painful than trying to swim against the proverbial current.

Makaria laughs her cracked, whistling laugh, banging a spoon on one of the large copper pots she's assembled. The kitchen looks like a raven's roost. "Anyone else? You think that I, a daughter of Hades himself, can simply transfer my powers? No, no. Only my line can preserve the link. Father wouldn't trust anyone else."

"It's an honor, really, though it doesn't always feel that way," Kalum says with a sympathetic look at his mother.

An uncomfortable silence falls upon them.

"So, I suppose that I'll have to visit the villa on my own then. It's not far from here, I'm told," Christabel says.

"No, not far at all," Kalum replies. His dark eyes hold hers for just a moment too long. He's hiding something. Or he's embarrassed. "I can show you the way," he adds.

The realization is not unexpected, but it is still a disappointment. Christabel has spent the better part of the last ten years working to repair the relations between gods and monsters. There is no innocent side, no honorable preservation, among them. If there is anything she's learned, it's that everyone has another motivation. No one is in it for the sheer good of the matter or the betterment of the world.

Everyone wants something.

"I don't have many details," says Christabel. "But I'm told that up until about a month ago the Villa de Valeria was uninhabited."

"Yes," says Kalum. "They are not quite our nearest neighbors, but we had certainly considered the place a few decades away from a ruin. The previous owners were the sorts of people who threw orgies every Wednesday, and to be honest we were quite glad when they finally left town for Luxembourg."

Christabel does not want to ask, but Makaria continues anyway.

"They were worse than vampires," she says in between cracking a long root in half with her hands and then tossing it absently into the boiling pot next to her. *Mantequero.* Manticores. All those human and animal heads all bobbing up and down and sucking and biting. Quite a mess and a nuisance."

A few decades before, when she hadn't known Hermes, Christabel might have blushed. But now she explores such ribaldry through both an academic lens and a personal one. Though Kalum is delicious to look upon, and he does have the most delicate fingers, she finds herself retreating into her mind to study the facts. Just like Worth, she's learned the hard way that romantic dalliances are dangerous diversions.

"Manticores were not part of the Treaty of Thule," Christabel says, citing her most prized publication to date, if one can call a treaty a publication. "They are infamously difficult to work with and have no notions of propriety, let alone allegiance."

"They weren't always so bad," says Makaria. "But, alas, you're right. We were glad to see them go, and so were the locals. Too many flocks and stragglers ending up dead. You'd think they would have been less brazen about it."

"Regardless of the manticores, my very esteemed hosts, I worry that I am losing time. As I said, a friend of mine has been in possession of this new landlord of the Villa de Valeria a long while, and I am most anxious to see this through," Christabel says. She hopes she cuts an impressive figure, drawing the power of her light around her, but she is doubtful. "I am waiting for my friends, though I fear they are somewhat delayed, so it is up to me to scout the area."

Makaria frowns, drawing her dark hair over her shoulder like a shy maiden. "Of course, of course. We should have considered that you were pressed for time. I will simply have to lend you my Kalum for a while."

For his part, Kalum looks just as shocked as Christabel feels.

"Mother…" He might even be afraid, judging by the tremor in his voice.

"It's not necessary," says Christabel. "He has already been more than kind on the matter. I hadn't anticipated front door service at the airport."

Outside, the wind picks up, bringing with it the heady scent of the ocean churning the refuse of a thousand years. It reminds Christabel of her time with Dr. Frye, and she wishes she were back on that shore with Jenn the Selkie. She also wishes that Nerissa and Ophaniel and whoever else might be on their way would arrive. This was supposed to be their safe house.

With the breeze comes another scent, honeyed and musky, followed by four beautiful butterflies. No, moths. It's nighttime. There would never be butterflies at night.

Christabel knows from her studies that these are *Graesllsia isabellae* and the smell is asphodel. She is about to ask a question about the smell and the unlikely guests when Makaria lets out a gasp.

"Oh, no."

That isn't exactly what she says, for she switches to Greek for her exclamation, and the little butterflies alight on her shoulders, then begin crawling up her face. Christabel realizes it ought to be a pleasant sight, and yet it disturbs her. The smell is too strong, the moths almost frenzied.

"I thought he was just being difficult," Makaria says, as if conversing with the butterflies. "He's always up in arms about some insult or another, and when he said that it was Artemis, well, I simply couldn't..." She groans, talking to the wall, now. "And then she comes in and I can practically see Hermes' hands all over her!"

Instead of making eye contact, or offering any sliver of an explanation, Kalum regards his mother with growing unease. He wrings his hands. His eyes widen. He takes a step forward, gently, as if he were trying to prevent a frightened colt from rearing.

Then words come out of Makaria's mouth. It is a beautiful voice, Christabel cannot deny it, and it rumbles from the very bottom of the worlds.

It is the voice of death.

My sister's daughter is captured. They will take her; they will bleed her. There is no room for her down here. They will leave her to oblivion, undying and unliving.

"Grandfather," says Kalum, falling to his knees before his mother. "What is this?"

I told my daughter, your mother, that there were plots winding their way in the above world. That they would wait until I could not interfere, for it is winter and I cannot travel. My wife lights the other side of the world. But Apollo's sister...she carries the guilt we all do and was brought under false pretenses.

"What do we do?" Christabel has not asked such a question in time out of mind. Typically, people ask her this question, as she has the gift for prioritization and action, a combination she finds most creatures—be they god, human, or monsters—simply do not possess. But she has never been involved in a drama of this magnitude, with true gods and goddesses battling for their survival.

Ah, Monoceros.

She hates that name.

Famed light. You and my niece Artemis are born of a similar light. The same melody of the universe formed eons ago. You will find your answers, and you will find your betrayal there. Your friends hasten toward you.

"I will stay with Mother," Kalum says suddenly, as if it is the most courageous decision of his lifetime. But the words are hardly out of his mouth when Makaria's eyes light up with a deep blue flame, and her teeth glow with the effort of the power coursing through her.

You will help the Monoceros. She is your opposite. She is bright. She is brave. But she will need measures of the other to survive. You do not fight a creature of blood and bone, nor of ichor and bramble.

The enemy of the stars comes to us now.

* * *

The "enemy of the stars" makes little sense to Christabel, but then again, she long ago realized that sense does not equal her reality. Nothing about her friends, nothing about her existence, makes a great deal of logic. She is forever a living conflict, drawn to desire, and yet prevented from sating herself. A human form and an animal form, living together in harmony, yet always lingering like an unresolved chord...

She has done brave things before. She has put herself before a great beast consuming the souls of supernatural beings. She has tried to sacrifice herself for the love of her life—she can say that now, if only to herself—and then she walked away from him because she knew it was the only way toward a semblance of happiness.

Now the brumal expanse of her heart quivers with anticipation and worry, and again with the thundering chorus of joy that comes with impending battle.

The pieces begin to arrange themselves in her mind as she follows Kalum down a moonlit path toward the famed Villa de Valeria. Vivienne is most certainly more than what she seems, for her part in this strange conjunction cannot be mere chance. If the powers that be wanted her dead, it most certainly would have happened sooner. And why involve Artemis? And now, Hades? This location could not have been an accident.

How long had the orchestration gone on? And how old, exactly, was Vivienne?

"You know, I don't think there's much of a difference between lamias and sylphs," Christabel says out loud to Kalum. She has been silent until now, mostly out of respect for his trembling and muttering, but she cannot take it any longer. So she turns to the subject of some of their academic correspondence. "From a mythological perspective, anyway. They'd both be classified as quite similar."

"There are a dozen other topics we could cover, but I'll allow it. I'd always chalked up lamias as daughters of Medusa, or some such," says Kalum. "But I suppose you may be correct."

"Certainly you have read Ovid," Christabel says, the entirety of her opinion of this man resting on his reply.

"Of course, I have."

"Good. Then I will permit you to stay."

She realizes how flirtatious she sounds, and so she barrels through the conversation.

"I'm trying to bring the story here. This 'enemy of the stars' you mentioned. Why would they want Vivienne? Well, Vivienne calls herself a night sylph, which is a rather vague term. She is, more precisely, a *nymph*. Likely the product of a god and or goddess and a mortal being, I had just not considered that she was of Greek origin. She could even be a lesser demigod. Her power appears centered around the cold, and frost in particular, which is made of water. So she could certainly be a *naiad*."

"But your friend Nerissa is a snake, is she not? A gorgon?"

Christabel sees his logic and knows it is in error, but it is still fun to watch him squirm after the clues. "Her middle name is *Melusine.* Which isn't even clever if she was trying to *hide,* now that I think about it. Nerissa is a character from *The Merchant of Venice*, which has no significance other than the character pretends to be a man named Stephano at once point, but the etymology of the name is of Greek derivation and means 'sea nymph.'"

"But she's a lamia. A scaly thing."

"Scales do not make a snake. She bleeds blueish green, like an octopus. And Nymphs don't have to be beautiful by human standards, Kalum. When they do not follow such shapes, they are labeled monsters. But I spent a good deal of my life researching these very situations. Vivienne—whose name is laughingly a reference to Arthur's Lady of the Lake and, I should say, well after her time—is only considered a monster for her past. She lived a life of sorrow and blood for a long while before beginning... although there is a good deal of wind to her work, as well. Which is odd, considering it is something most often observed in demigods and the like and she is very powerful. Or at least, I recall her being so. I was so young at the time, you understand, having very little in the way of notes."

Sorrow and blood. "They are powerful, connected beings, Vivienne and Nerissa. And if Artemis, and Hades are involved, then it makes me think of what your grandfather said – something about being guilty for misdeeds. There are so many, though. So, so many."

Another moth crosses Christabel's path, and she stares at it.

Artemis. Leda.

Enemy of the stars.

Cygna.

Ophaniel sits at the top of his roof and complains that the Cygna constellation is out of line...

A letter from Nerissa.

"What is it?" Kalum stops and turns, looking Christabel in the eyes.

"The enemy of the stars. Cygna...but I had thought...and it would mean...oh, heavens, Kalum, we've got to hurry up."

14

A PROMISE FROM A BUTTERFLY

Artemis is beautiful in the way a mountain is beautiful. Cold like the ocean is cold. Vengeful like a bubbling pit of lava. When the gods first realized Vivienne, albeit by another name, into the world, it was only Artemis for whom she lived. Her entire life revolved around the goddess's compass.

Unlike her own wispy figure, the goddess was all thickness and roundness and power. She towered over everyone else, dwarfed even her brother Apollo. Artemis was a hunter, the power of a trained predator deep in her bones and her every movement. Vivienne—though then they called her Aura—always felt that Artemis kept her around as a point of contrast. Look at Aura; she is so thin and underfed, her breasts so small, her bones so sharp. For the child of a Titan, she should be grand, but she is only frail and full of breezes.

Vivienne can't remember why she said what she did, or what drew her to boast of her own beauty. She knows she was happy with Artemis, that she never wanted for anything. The hunt was her life, and she knew only contentment as she drifted upon the winds and chased the fleetest prey.

But she spoke the words. She had too much to drink. She was soaking herself in the water, naked with the hunting party, and she teased Artemis for her large breasts, teased her for the thickness of her limbs. "It would be difficult for a lover to encircle an oak when they can have a willow."

Artemis did not laugh.

She was furious. But Aura felt as if she had a right to challenge the goddess. Aura was, after all, the daughter of a Titan, too. Why should she not have her fun?

Then Artemis spoke.

And Nemesis listened.

"Behold your goddess," Bastille says, holding out his arms like a circus conductor. "Oh, Aura. It took so long to bring all of this together. Ages and ages, my dear. But you remember, don't you? You remember Cygna? This makes so much sense now, doesn't it?"

Artemis hangs her head, dark hair coiling down her bare chest. They have made her a mockery. And even Vivienne, who has plenty of distaste for the goddess, feels the pain of it. The wrongness of it.

She had told Nadine the story, mostly. As if Aura had been her mother. Because it was safer to have that distance. For centuries, Vivienne supposes, she even began to believe it. Separating herself from the pain was a way of enduring.

Vivienne is trying hard to put the pieces together, working even harder to dredge up the right memories and not the worst memories. Because there was a time when she was…not Aura, not Vivienne, but a creature much worse and baser. A justified monster, perhaps, but a horrific one. Her eyes stream with tears.

She feels clammy. She is frozen, though. And the metal at her wrists bites into her skin, and she can feel that it is cold, which is so strange. All her life, the cold and the wind have been her friends; but now, when she could use them most, they are outside of her grasp.

Bastille is looking at her through his strange, hooded orange eyes.

"Why am I here?" Vivienne asks at last, finding it the best of her options. Not for the first time she wishes Nerissa was here with her. She would have a clever phrase. Hell, even the unicorn would be preferable to being alone.

Then she appears. Out of nothing. Cygna. A mortal, yes. But cut into the world as if in glass. She wears rings on all her fingers, bright silvery trinkets that match what Bastille carries on his person. Her hair is shorn short, square, at her chin, her clothes practical. If not for her strange sharpness, and that she stepped into the room from a black hole in the wall, she would be almost unremarkable.

Cygna looks disappointed, puffing out her bottom lip. "Come now, it hasn't been that long, Aura, has it? Am I that forgettable? Aside from you, I may have been a true competitor if not for my pestilent sister."

Vivienne stares at Cygna's face; tries to remove the modern trappings. Longer hair, a lighter shade. Homespun, perhaps. A diadem on her head. Long, red-tipped fingers…

"Philonoe," Vivienne says, reaching back through the scarred lines of her mind, the compartments she'd burned away for centuries. "But how are…how are you *alive?*"

Philonoe was a daughter of Leda and King Tyndareus, sister to Helen, Clytemnestra, Pollux, and Castor. A foot-note in history, but a devoted priestess of Artemis. A mortal.

Yes, they had been together as friends. Vivienne used to plait her hair.

"Ah, but that is the crux of the matter, isn't it?" Cygna smiles widely, showing her even teeth. She is remarkably well-preserved for someone so old, a mortal thousands of years in the making. "Do you remember that night? When I found you? What I said to you?"

Vivienne does not remember the words, no. But she knows the night that Cygna speaks of. The name makes more sense now; she is a daughter of Leda. She should have made the connection.

"Artemis remembers."

Artemis struggles in her alabaster prison, and Vivienne notices that even her hands are bound. Clever. Gypsum, alabaster, the prized component of the Titans. The only thing that might keep an Olympian down. In immense measures, of course. Which Vivienne suspects is below her, as well.

"Tell her, Artemis. Tell her what happened," Cygna presses.

"I do not need to hear it," Vivienne says, fingers shaking, aching. Her body, bereft of its magic, is like an open wound. "I know what happened. I remember Dionysus. I remember the horror. I remember…"

"After you killed your child," Cygna says lightly, to Vivienne, "I came to you in your sickbed, and I promised you we would give Artemis her due. After spiriting your son away, of course. I promised you and promised you and promised you."

That part, Vivienne does not recall. Truth be told she remembers only the barest of glimmers of Cygna, of Philonoe, at all. She was mortal, then. And mortals, at that point in her long life, did little to impress her. They were like shadows, little butterflies flitting in and out of existence. How could she remember a promise from a butterfly?

But she remembers her sons. And the blood of her child on her lips. And the feeling of Dionysus ravaging her body, the blood flowing between her legs, and the chill wind that took her heart.

"By then," Cygna continues, "Artemis had given me her gift. As she did to my sister Bolina, her gift at the hand of Apollo. *Immortality*. It seemed like such a boon at first. But time went on and, oh, I tried so hard to kill myself. I flayed myself; I burned myself; I threw my body to snakes and manticores and beasts of any kind, and still, nothing."

"Until she found me," Bastille says. He has been so quiet that Vivienne starts at his voice. There is warmth in his tone now. "Until she met another who had been wronged by the Olympians."

There was no doubt that the Olympians were wretched, warped, disturbed individuals. It was no surprise they made enemies along the way. But Cygna and Bastille weren't just looking for revenge; they were looking for utter annihilation.

"I'm surprised it took you that long to find someone else," Vivienne says, finding her inner calm. "The list is long and exhaustive. You must have had certain criteria to narrow your options so. And a very, very long time wasted."

Bastille grins. "Oh, but you weren't easy to find, Aura. And we had our minds on a particular Olympian, and you had reinvented yourself so many times we weren't sure it was still you. Besides, we needed to try the magic dampening on someone powerful enough. The metals we found," he holds up his hand, "protect and preserve, depending on the form and function."

"But you've captured me," Vivienne says. "You've brought me here. And there. And everywhere in between. You bargained with Barqan, you ordered me to perplex the streets of Cairo with death masks, and now you've kept me chained for another decade. Why? If you wanted my help, why didn't you merely ask?" As if she would have agreed.

Cygna gives Vivienne a pitying look. "What is a decade or two to you, my dear? But a blip on the radar of life. A mere gadfly on the back of an enormous wildebeest. In Cairo, your powers proved too strong. You made contact with the lamia and your other friends. I couldn't bring you in on the plan until you were somewhat cowed. So you could understand where the power truly lay now."

There are nearly one million words in the English language, and over the millennia Vivienne du Lac has learned a great many of them. She has spoken Greek, Etruscan, Scythian, Phoenician, and every Latinate language known to man, as well as a sprinkling of Basque, Old Norse, and Finnish, her personal favorite. But there is one word that particularly bothers her. And Cygna uses it with the precision of a woman who knows a great deal more information about Vivienne than she had expected. *Cowed.* For the first time in an age, she imagines pulling out Cygna's heart, freezing it and laughing as it shatters into little flecks of red snow.

"You were *extremely* powerful," Bastille corrects, taking out his glasses and cleaning the lenses of one and then the other. "And quite devoted to your friends and the mortal world. But as you can see, they are a comedy of errors. We've been keeping an eye on them, to make sure, and they're still in London caring for that winged thing. And even if they do reach us, we have a variety of protections in place. As you have learned, we've refined our approach."

Winged thing?

Vivienne keeps her face impassive. Never has Bastille given her news. Not even a whisper. She hasn't even known for certain if her friends are alive.

"What the basilisk is trying to say," Cygna says, leaning on the alabaster plinth grown around the goddess, "is that we want your help yes, perhaps. You weren't just given the gifts of your progenitors, the power of wind, but in Zeus's curse, you were given another. Water. Though, thankfully it doesn't seep out of your breasts like in the stories. What a ridiculous notion."

Artemis won't look at her. Vivienne wonders if she knows what happened; she must. But what of the other part? How after her rape, after Vivienne devoured her own children, Zeus came to her and cursed her.

Or so he said.

So everyone thought.

Yes, Zeus stood before her and shouted his decree. He banished her from Greece, he threw down thunder from Olympus and made her drink a rank potion that tasted of salt and brine because she had dared to challenge Artemis.

When Zeus left, and Aura felt nothing, she remained rooted to the ground, shaking, bewildered. Still mad, yes, but with a clarity that only the fear of a god such as he could engender.

Hermes appeared out of the brush with a ram by his side. He explained that he had switched the draught from Zeus, and what she had sipped was only a mixture he'd concocted from saltwater and ram's blood.

He brought her to a shallow pool. He soothed her skin with salves; he combed the blood and burrs from her hair. He sang softly the whole time but said nothing more for a long while.

The sun was rising again when Aura began to untangle the webs of her own heart, and Hermes sat with her while she wept. He gathered her tears in a vial and said quiet words over it, and then told her to drink of it. Her stomach burned with the power of the drink, but then it cooled her mind and soul.

"You will never be whole again," he said, "as so many of us who are ruined by my family. But I will give you something new. I like to change the threads of our story when I can, and I see in you a fellow wanderer, and a conveyor of souls, though perhaps in a different way. Sleep, Aura, sleep, and awake knowing you have as many chances in life as you can imagine. You can rise anew, make for yourself a new name, a new life, a new purpose. It may take a thousand years, but you will find it."

And now Vivienne sits at the crux of a chance in life.

She knows what is coming next.

These sorts of beings—whether they are gods or not, and whether they see themselves as good or not—want something from her. Want her power. Want her mind. Want her experience. It's one of the reasons she struck out on her own so long ago, why she turned her work toward more mortal goals along with monster rehabilitation.

If they were ever really monsters to begin with.

She thinks, not for the first or last time, that they should reconsider the meaning of the word.

Vivienne does not deny she harbors anger toward Artemis; more than anger. She holds a deep, soul-aching fury. But she has healed it with time, though the scar still stands. And she is not alone. Cygna is not wrong that the Olympians left nothing but death in their wake. But this? Were they real allies, they would never have resorted to making her stoop.

They are afraid of her, just as she was fearful of Barqan without his shackles.

"We want your help," Cygna says. "You can help us banish Artemis forever. And then, one by one, her brothers and sisters. To the Void. To the endless nothing. They will not sleep. They will not breathe. But they will be surrounded by blackness and know every agonizing minute."

15

FIRE AND FURY

Nerissa lives in a world built on overextended neurons, adrenaline gone mad, and the constant sensation that the very fabric of her physical and arcane self is being pulled to the edge of consciousness, reason, and madness.

She is keenly aware that she is as close to death as she will ever be—or has been, for that matter. And that is no small task. She can recall dozens of fights, altercations, blemishes, and even wars that have left her broken and bruised, but none of them felt like this.

It is as if she is on two planes of existence.

No, maybe three.

There is the corporeal world of Earth that she knows well. Her body, writhing and wriggling in Dr. Plover's office, remains there save for two left arms. They are clasped together—she can feel her phantom fingers grasping in a death grip—somewhere colder and darker and emptier than any oblivion she has ever dreamed of, and somehow it seeps through her consciousness into this third world.

A dream world.

Not the Fae. She would know that. She has run from it so many times that it's almost as familiar as London by now, though, perhaps, easier to navigate.

And she cannot explain it for the life of her, but in this in-between place, she feels closer to Vivienne than she's ever been. She can almost smell the myrtle and honeysuckle that always seems to cling to her; she keeps half expecting to see a shadow of her or hear her voice.

But where is Nerissa now?

She has no eyes to close or open, no body to feel directly. It is as if she lives inside of the pain, inhabiting the pathways and doorways woven together in her very being.

Perhaps that isn't so off. Nerissa imagines Kit might have a similar explanation—she is either coping with the pain by creating a sub-stratum inside her consciousness or else she has truly gone mad.

Though, and not for the first time in her life, Nerissa feels as if madness is merely a moniker for what dull minds cannot understand. And that it might be a relief.

The pain moves through her like lightning, over and over again, but does not increase in its severity. Nerissa wonders if it's possible to increase in severity at this point.

It is then, just as she feels closer to the answer to her current state of consciousness, that she becomes aware of a sharp smell. It's spicy and vegetal and reminds her of Cairo. It takes her a moment to realize what it is since she isn't smelling through her nose or any other discernible orifice.

Then she *sees* for the first time since leaving her physical body. But it feels more like a projection. Nerissa knows what dreams feel like, understands the meanderings of her own subconscious; this is not such an occurrence.

She is in a glade, surrounded by bay laurel on every side. Clusters of the plant grow what she would assume would be waist-high if she had such a vantage point. It's difficult to tell.

The sky is a strange shade of robin's egg blue, shifting from a greener version to a more azure hue the longer she lingers on it. The ground is covered in moss and birds fly overhead.

And there is a man.

No, not a man.

A god.

Nerissa is tired of gods by now, but at least she's got the wherewithal to know she's in the presence of one. It has caused some amount of distress and embarrassment in the past to think of them as anything other. But to her credit, they do have a habit of concealing their power and wreaking havoc on the general public.

However, this god is unlike any of the gods she's seen before. He is not concealed in an underworld as Serket and Heqet were. He springs out of this strange Earth—and she is sure it is still Earth, somehow, or at least a strong projection of one—and she sees that he is *indeed* the sun.

Apollo. He stands in perfect, pure nudity, every muscle and vein carved with precision across his body, every golden hair placed with expert care. His hair curls over his bronzed forehead then falls in longer locks down his back. Somehow, though he wears absolutely no adornment, he seems gaudy in his presence; too much gold and glitter for Nerissa. For the first time since vanishing from the pain, she is glad her real eyes aren't looking. She might feel nauseated.

"Daughter of Titans," he says, and his voice is not anywhere near as impressive as Nerissa expects. Perhaps it's the transference. He sounds quite ordinary, but by the cadence of his words, she suspects he thinks the effect is much grander. So is the plight of many a naked man, she imagines.

"Nerissa is good enough," she responds, though she's not

sure how. Her voice comes from behind her. Or below her. It's hard to tell without ears.

Apollo looks confused, his glimmering exterior turning oddly wooden as he takes a step closer. "You're a nymph," he says. "You're the daughter of Titans."

"I never thought of it that way," she says. The conversation is a welcome change from constant pain. "I just figured I was the unwanted chaff of some ill-informed coupling."

"You don't know your parentage?"

"It's never really come up, but you're not the first one to ask. If it weren't for my friend Vivienne, I'd still be stalking the English Moors and sucking on anything with a pulse. It wasn't a pleasant life. It's more difficult now to get a decent meal, but it's significantly less exhausting."

"You befuddle me, creature."

"I befuddle myself on most days. But, as you say, I grew up without a family, and so I've had to make my own. How is that so strange? I am no monster, really; I am no worse than you."

Apollo stops and runs a hand through his shimmering golden hair. He appears most frustrated with Nerissa, but she is fatigued and in a great deal of pain.

"I think I'm dying," she says, "so unless you have something to help me through this, I'd prefer to be left alone rather than made to feel guilty about a family genealogy that is irrelevant to my present situation."

"I am the god of healing."

"I'm aware."

"I can help you."

"My arms are severed from the rest of me, and I think they're in a void somewhere."

"That isn't terribly specific."

"I'm afraid in my current state being specific is difficult."

"You really don't want to know?"

"Know what?"

"Your parentage."

Apollo doesn't seem to want to let this go, and Nerissa is losing patience, if patience can exist in mere consciousness. Or dreaming. Or both.

Give a little sweetness if you want something in return. It was one of Vivienne's better pieces of advice, along with making sure one's underpinnings were always clean and to avoid licking people's hands when proffered.

Since Nerissa hasn't yet decided if she's dreaming or not but has accepted that she is probably dying, she figures that Apollo really wants to tell her. He's a gossip, as she has always suspected. One who shines on everyone and sees everything, after all. He probably revels in bringing light to dark places.

"I am Nerissa Melusine Waldemar, or at least that is what I have called myself since I could form a coherent thought," she says at last. "I don't see how knowing my parents could change anything."

Apollo looks absolutely elated. He presses his delicate fingertips together just below his nose, accentuating just how shockingly symmetrical his features are. It is alarming, Nerissa thinks, looking into a face without flaw. Nothing about him can be improved. And that is almost sad.

"How delightful," Apollo says. "It's as if you knew all along."

"Pardon? I'm dying."

"Doubtful."

"What?"

The god sighs dismissively. "I knew you for a chthonic the moment I saw you. *Dying* isn't in your vocabulary, so you can stop blubbering about that. Your mother's name was Melinoë. Melusine is so very close, isn't it? Regardless, she had a tryst with one of those flighty river gods, and along you came. I believe there was some discussion as to what to do. You do realize Melinoë is a daughter of Persephone, so we're practically cousins."

He says this in a manner that does not indicate any such familial relations but rather him trying mightily to make the situation brighter than it is. Or more fascinating. It is neither.

"I'm a snake," says Nerissa.

"Of course you are. Your father was probably Archeron; at least that is my guess. So he flowed through the mortal realm and into the Underworld, which would explain how he met your mother, I suppose. I never asked. It is ever difficult to keep the Potamoi apart from one another. It's likely that you get your...ah, looks from him."

"Why are you saying I can't die?"

"Because you were born of the rivers of the Underworld and a nymph steeped in the River Styx. A mad bird, really, but a friendly one. I suppose you ended up lost in the shuffle at some point. It happens. I wouldn't take it personally."

"I don't."

This new information feels like bubbles inside of Nerissa's consciousness. Or like bees buzzing. She doesn't wish to show that it has somehow changed her, but she knows it has. She feels it in her marrow.

"Not that you aren't still a monster, by some definition," Apollo says with a yawn. "But aren't we all?"

"Can you heal me? I'm in a great deal of pain."

"I can heal anything I can put my hands on, and some things I can't. But first, we must locate those missing appendages of yours, which may prove difficult. But now that you're here, I should be able to trace them back. Give me a moment."

Apollo claps his hands, and a white raven careens from the flock in the sky and lands on his shoulder. He leans back and whispers in its ear, and the thing tilts its head side to side as if listening. Nerissa has always liked ravens and birds in general, feeling a kind of kinship to them, but she is distracted and doesn't ask any more questions.

What would Vivienne say? Nerissa has built a whole story for herself, a place in the cosmos: a lonely monster on the Moors rescued by a gallant nymph, noble of mind and soul who turned from her dark ways.

It still smells of honeysuckle. Why does it smell of honeysuckle?

The white raven flies off, and Nerissa stays for an indeterminate amount of time as Apollo goes stiff as a statue, eyes closed, hands pressed to his ears, brow furrowed in concentration. She tries to push out the questions and concerns from her thoughts, but all she is currently is thoughts, and it is therefore impossible to run from them.

So she thinks of Vivienne. And she wonders that she has never asked about her background. What is a sylph, anyway? As Christabel believes, all monsters stem from the divine, regardless of the pantheon. They have never belonged, not really. And Worth, least of all. And Ophaniel…

Apollo shudders and straightens up, his eyes shooting open. They are white through and through, no sign of an iris or a pupil, but the look of surprise is unmistakable.

"You cannot kill a god," he whispers. "But you can trap it indefinitely."

"What's that?"

Apollo begins to pace back and forth, pulling in his bottom lip. It makes him look like a toddler. A gleaming, naked, physically perfect toddler. "You said a void."

"I did. But then you had to go and drag up all the sordid details of my chthonic past, didn't you?"

"I am going to have to…oh, I hate this part. I can't believe

Artemis would be this stupid...I can't believe...Cygna! That goat."

There is a good deal more muttering, but Nerissa doesn't have time to process it because Apollo bull rushes her. That's the only explanation she can give. Whatever presence of hers exists is suddenly thrust out and squeezed into a thin membrane of being and then stretched, pulled, and popped back into consciousness.

She feels warm hands on her face, feels the sun's first rays of morning melting her cold heart, casting its light on her skin. Her skin! She can feel her skin! Something wet touches her lips, and it is sweet, and she usually is more of a savory person, but drinks it down to the dregs.

"Nerissa, it's time to wake up."

It's Apollo's voice, but calmer this time. Grounded. Muffled.

She opens her eyes and sees Apollo, or at least a version of him, standing beside her in Dr. Plover's townhouse. He is a little taller than Kit and wears clothing that was fashionable half a century ago. But it's classic enough that she supposes it passes.

In the light of the mortal world Apollo's hair is dark brown shot with copper, and his skin is a rich olive tone. His eyes are blue rimmed with green, and his teeth are so star-tlingly white that they are disturbing when he smiles.

Still, Nerissa is not dead. And she is in a manageable amount of pain. And she is incredibly hungry.

Those in the room gasp at his appearance and Nerissa's sudden awakening.

"Hello, everyone," says Apollo. "I'm Apollo. I'm here to help you save the world."

OF TINY, WELL-DRESSED BEINGS

When Worth returns to the living room, a cup of coffee in his hand, still thinking about Christabel, Nerissa is sleeping. But she is not quiet for long, yet in the short time she's unconscious, Worth observes the lamia as her eyes glow from beneath her lids. It's an ungodly sight—or perhaps a godly one, he is still trying to figure those sorts of things out—and it leaks down her cheeks like golden rain. Then comes a heady smell like Mediterranean cooking, that spicy bite of bay leaf he's always associated with such cuisine.

Dr. Plover tilts his head this way and that, and says, "This was not what I had anticipated."

"I thought you were a good doctor," Kit says, heat in her voice turning it almost to a growl. She's going a bit feral, and Worth can't blame her. He'd felt the same about someone else before.

Don't think about her. I don't like it when you think about her.

Well, I can't very well help it. I think she's the only thing keeping me here, old chap. Christabel is very likely the only thing

134

preventing me from going the way of a half-remembered melody in your head, and I'm not particularly keen on all those loose ends.

You were *you* for a long time. Not long in angel years, but long in immortal years, to be sure. I suppose it'll wear off eventually.

Worth is surprised that Ophaniel sounds almost sad about that. But now there is a great deal of screaming, and the presence of Ophaniel rears back within Worth, and he staggers into a buffet table, knocking glassware off. He doesn't have time to react, however, because Nerissa sits up bolt straight with a blast of light, her arms out before her as if preparing for a blow.

Arms. Two arms. She is back in her glamour.

One arm is quite familiar. The other is made of some metal material. Bronze, perhaps?

Oh, and there is also a man standing before them. He's wearing the strangest conglomeration of clothes Worth has ever seen, so bizarre that even his limited sartorial taste is offended. It isn't that the man isn't handsome—he is that and then some. Worth is quite positive the man standing before them is the most attractive person of human form he has ever beheld. The eyes could be no more almandine; the hair no more perfectly curled; the skin no more sweetly curved and kissed by the sun.

But the uninvited guest is wearing a toga. And over the toga, a Regency-era jacket in vivid puce, tied with a thick red kerchief about the neck. He also has a crown of ornately twisted leaves in his hair, studded now and again with stones of varying shades.

And a cape. He is wearing a velvet cape. It is green. And it appears formed from moss. And not in a good way.

The man has omitted shoes.

Nerissa is coughing and hacking now, however, and that takes the attention away from the guest. She is shivering from foot to fang, and Kit is putting her arms around her and is she crying?

Worth is feeling a bit off at the moment. Ten years mostly shoved to the back of Ophaniel's mind like an afterthought, and now he's thrust again into this emotional torrent. Usually, Nerissa would be there to comfort him in such a situation, bastion of unfeeling frigidity that she often is. But now she is holding Kit back, and letting the *kitsune* stroke her hair, and Dr. Plover is hopping around them, trying to get questions in.

But then the guest speaks, and everyone falls silent.

"HELLO!"

His voice is musical, arresting, in the way French horns come unbidden in an ill-conceived symphony.

"MY NAME IS APOLLO. I HAVE-"

"Not so loud," Nerissa says through gritted teeth. "You'll wake the whole neighborhood."

Apollo looks around, though Worth doesn't think he is in any way concerned about his behavior. Still, rolling his eyes, he takes a deep breath and tries again.

"Greetings, you of mortal derivation."

"We're not mortals," Dr. Plover says. "Sir? Lord? I'm…"

"Not mortals?" Apollo tries, but he does not seem prepared for such an occasion.

"I'm a celestial," Worth says, adding, "Mostly. Most days. For much of the day. Right now."

"It isn't very straightforward," Nerissa adds. "But these are my friends, and they are here to help you."

"We are?" Kit and Worth and Dr. Plover say this all at once.

Nerissa holds out a calming hand. Not the shining one, the regular one. "Apollo found me wandering around. I was being torn apart after those *things* got to me."

"The bleaknesses," says Kit with a jut of her chin. No one will argue the point, Worth is quite certain.

"Yes. *Those*. I was wandering around, likely headed to the Underworld. My Underworld. You see—"

"You're one of Styx's progeny," Dr. Plover says lightly. "I could have told you that. A lamia doesn't simply appear out of nowhere; nor does Medusa. We all begin as something. Well, except for me. I have always been a bird."

"And a fine bird," says Apollo.

Worth is worried for a moment that this will devolve into a long flirtation before anyone understands what is happening.

Thankfully, Kit, as usual, retrieves the conversational reins.

"Why does Nerissa have a metal arm?" The *kitsune* is cradling the metal contraption, examining it, and the lamia isn't concerned with this overt show of affection. "It's very bright and doesn't match the rest of her."

Your friends confuse me.

You are not alone, Ophaniel.

Apollo takes a deep breath, but Worth can tell this is simply an affectation. The god doesn't need to breathe.

"Your friend Nerissa came to me. Rather, I found her, ambling her way down to the River Styx to cross that final border. Her pain was so great it enveloped her like thick silk, nay, like a feathered corona of raven wings, prepared to escort her—"

"I almost died. He found me. He fixed my arms with this contraption. It's confusing." She takes a sharp breath, wincing. "The bleaknesses are from a bitch named Cygna who has Artemis. And probably Vivienne."

Nerissa's interruption makes Worth stifle a grin. It is good to see her again.

* * *

Kit is suffering. And yet it is sweet. She felt the last wisps of doubt leave, that thin veil between amusement and slight repulsion for the lamia, replaced with love, but now she sits at its precipice of this veritable cliff. Kit was positive Nerissa was going to die, or else be sundered from her forever, and that thought sent her agile mind into a thousand dark alleyways.

She resigned herself to it.

But now, Kit stares directly into Nerissa's eyes and the lamia does not look away. She also does not move Kit's hand from her own. Cold though it is, the mechanism is a wonder, but Kit isn't pretending that she's holding on to Nerissa for rational reasons.

The bird doctor is trying fiercely to talk to the man-boy god. What kind of god looks like that, Kit can't help but wonder. He should be at least a foot taller. As it is, he looks like an overgrown prepubescent boy, with distractingly chiseled features. And clothing that even Kit knows is out of place.

"We've known for some time that Cygna was a threat," says the man-god, brushing his unnaturally perfect curls from his abnormally smooth brow. If he's trying to pass for human, he's doing a miserable job of it. "She has written scathing notes to we Olympians for a while now, but after a time one gets rather immune to the charms of a mortal threat."

"This must tie back to Cairo," Nerissa says, and Kit feels her lean into her touch, half-thinking. It makes Kit so glad she wants to yip. But she does not. Generally speaking, even the most progressive among immortals don't appreciate such animal responses. "Vivienne was being used to craft masks, masks that granted people visages and powers often attributed to them—and paying for items not in coin but with stones. But then they found something they needed, and they were gone. We lost track of them."

"Christabel thought they had gone aquatic," Kit said. "You know, on the seas. As a rule, most of us struggle to keep our gifts about us on a good day. But having them afloat would mean it was even more difficult to track them using normal means."

"And you have all been preoccupied with Ophaniel. And me," says Worth, looking timid.

Kit doesn't like the idea of figuring out this puzzle. But then, she has sat on this problem for ages now. Christabel wrote to her on the matter once or twice, encouraging the *kistune* to tell Nerissa of her true feelings. But Kit has never really been in love before. She has never trusted people long enough for it.

And now they're closer to finding Vivienne than they have ever been.

And Nerissa loves Vivienne. And has loved her for centuries.

Kit feels herself pulling away. And Nerissa does not notice or does not seem to react when Kit is no longer holding the lamia's hand.

"What is so dangerous about this Cygna?" Dr. Plover lands across from the man-god, as if he wants a better look. "She's the source of this black magic?"

"She named herself after the constellation. After the place in the constellation where time itself folds in and vanishes. Where magic and life cease to exist in time. She had spoken of a desire to give us eternal damnation, in utter blackness— but sustained consciousness—forever." The boy man-god speaks the words as if he's giving a decree.

"Then why send the bleaknesses to us?" Nerissa asks.

"Because you have something she wants. Or someone. Or

she's just ready to destroy you." The boy man-god looks dubiously from face to face. "My guess is the one with the wings," he says at last, almost dismissively. "But you all have potential."

"Why bother with us at all? Even presuming that Vivienne is alive, there are dozens of other more powerful, far cleverer, beings out there."

"Perhaps you underestimate her. Vivienne…yes, the other one. Your friend. The one making the masks." The boy god's face darkens, mirth evaporating from his features. He looks terrifying. She cannot explain it other than that. In the absence of joy, his face is a horror.

The man-boy god sighs deeply. "Oh, Artemis. Oh, sister mine. You jealous twat."

* * *

They decide to retire for the evening, and Dr. Plover graciously offers his home. Of course, given his lavish, and expansive residence—large for a single man let alone a single bird—it shouldn't come as a surprise. But Kit gets the sense that it's a grander gesture than she can comprehend. One more of many odd social cues beyond her general understanding. These foreigners forever baffle her, even after almost a decade in London.

Kit is given a small room with a wide window, and she spends most of the dark hours looking outside while Nerissa speaks with Apollo and Dr. Plover about Vivienne.

Like most immortals, sleep is voluntary for her. Unlike most immortals, she has learned to like sleeping. It is a deep meditation for her, a time to reorder her often cluttered mind and rearrange her mental furniture.

But tonight, the furniture is too cluttered and heavy to move.

She worries about Nerissa so much that her chest hurts with it. She starts to write a note to her, to send across the house, but then she cannot find the right words. Everything comes out upside down.

Kit is half considering a nighttime walk when someone knocks softly on the door. Two steps toward it and she knows it's Worth. He smells of lavender with a hint of citrus.

"I saw the light," he says somewhat apologetically.

"You've got regular clothing on," she says. "I suppose the other one is resting?"

"I think the 'other one' is afraid of us."

"I do not blame him. We're a rather curious bunch. I never imagined a group of people would keep me among their ranks, but here I am. And no one asks me to leave anymore." She pauses and says, "I haven't had a chance to say, but it's quite nice having you here again. I must admit, I determined that the chance of seeing you again was closer to zero than a positive number. But here you are."

Worth's face pinches into a regretful, strained smile. "I don't know how long I'll have. Ophaniel has every capability of taking me over again. And I suppose we're one and the same, so I shouldn't be sad. And yet I am."

"Some people wish for reincarnation. I suppose you get two lives at once. In some ways that's lucky, you could say."

"You always have a way of phrasing things, my dear," Worth says, and there is genuine warmth in it. "But I'm not here to play philosopher. Tonight, I'd like to talk about a simpler matter. Well, two matters. And neither is simple. I'm trying to be polite, and I'm afraid I'm terrible at this whole business."

"You're even harder to follow than when you were Worth most of the time," she says to him. In times past she would have playfully hit him on the shoulder, but he is too angelic

141

for that now. "But I assume you want to talk to me about Nerissa."

Worth, as ever, is surprised by her candor. "How did you know?"

"You were looking at me quite intently during today's events. I had a feeling you were thinking about Christabel, and how you haven't seen her in the longest time, but you clearly can't be with her—though Ophaniel does like to talk about her—and you were looking at me the way you looked at her, once. Or at least her from a distance."

"I suppose I was a little jealous. Wistful. But also, in such matters, I like to think I have good experience to share with you."

"I know I should speak with her."

"You should. Why haven't you?"

"Because... because..." Kit tries to make the words come out sensical. But it's ever the struggle when the lamia is involved. "I can't even start to imagine what our lives would be like...together. I'm not the type of person to feel this way. I'm mercurial. I'm unpredictable. I don't like what it does to my narrative."

Worth laughs and Kit remembers just how much she used to like hearing that sound. Vibrant and low and boisterous. "Oh, Kit. Love isn't about fitting a narrative."

"I suppose you have all the answers to love, then."

"I most certainly do not. But I hypothesize that it's love that's kept me here, within Ophaniel, for this long. And love that has made me stronger. Love for Christabel, certainly. For Vivienne, too. And for Nerissa. And Alma. And yes, even you."

"Love feels like a complication none of us can afford right now."

"Love plays by its own rules. If a bleakness were to appear

right now and swallow you whole, and cast you into the forever darkness it promises...what would you do?"

"I'd find Nerissa's arms and bring them back."

"Kit."

She relents and finds herself biting back tears. This time the only words she has to say are not in Worth's language at all but in a tongue far older than even London itself.

Worth sighs and embraces her. She lets him. Though she also wants to bite him. When he speaks, it's in a low, lovely voice, that feels like silk on her soul.

"I know Nerissa might seem like she isn't the warmest of individuals, and if we're considering the temperature of her blood, I'm quite certain that would be true. But I've known her long enough to recognize when someone means more than a simple acquaintance. But I also know that in the centuries we've known one another, I've never seen her... well, happy. Despite everything, despite losing Vivienne, she is happy now. I think she has moved on."

"I'm afraid of what happens if we find Vivienne."

Saying it, finally, brings a weight off Kit's shoulders. She's been biting down on that fear since she first met Nerissa ten years ago.

Worth opens his arms again and Kit accepts the embrace. Outside the window, the sounds of late-night London rise, muffled against the pane.

They stand there for a while, listening to the noise around them, until Worth finally says, "So am I, Kit. So am I. That's what I came here to talk to you about."

"But I don't know Vivienne. I've never met her. I only know of her through Nerissa, and while she has kept some secrets to herself, it's abundantly clear that Vivienne is Nerissa's savior."

"In some ways, I suppose; but I do think it's also the other way around. Vivienne needs Nerissa, just as Nerissa needs

Vivienne. But when Nerissa told Vivienne her true feelings, well, it didn't go so well. You said before that the heart wants what it wants, and sometimes we cannot control things. I think Vivienne is likely sad that she never loved Nerissa in that way; guilty, perhaps, too."

"She has terrible taste," Kit says.

Worth's lips lengthen into a radiant smile. "Well, she was my paramour for quite some time, so I'll have to agree."

Kit almost laughs. Not quite. But she's open to the possibility that she might laugh again sometime soon. "But now?"

"My heart may never love again the way I love Christabel."

"And you're worried about seeing her again? And Vivienne? At the same time?"

Judging by the look of horror on Worth's face, it's just that. "Yes. Well, and I have a letter. For Christabel. If you'd give it to her…in case I'm not, well, me, by the time I see her. Or if things go south. There's just no way of knowing now."

He hands her a slim scroll, tied with a piece of white ribbon. It smells of fresh rain.

Kit nods. "I'd be happy to give it to her."

"I just hope it isn't too late."

"For what?"

Worth frowns. "For everything."

CRUISING

The Wolesley Hornet takes the curves toward the Villa de Valeria with ease. It's nighttime now, and Makaria is at home, but Kalum is in the driver's seat. Christabel notes how nervous he is, how he drums his fingers on the steering wheel in no discernable pattern at all, just a constant percussive inconvenience. She has clearly frightened him. Or the situation has. But then, seeing your mother channel Hades, your grandfather, with blue lights going out of her brain, can't have been easy.

"You didn't have to come," says Christabel, gently. She doesn't want to offend Kalum, but given the circumstances, she's not averse to it if it comes down to it. Dead weight on a mission like this isn't a good idea. "I could have driven myself or walked."

"Grandfather insisted," Kalum says. "And so do I."

"My friends are…well, they ought to have met us by now," she says. "Something has to have stopped them. So that means it might be just left to the two of us to interfere."

"I gathered as much," Kalum says.

The night air is soft on Christabel's skin, mildly humid

and smelling of salt. It makes her wish she could visit this place without the threat of obliteration hanging above her head. And that Kalum was a little less dim. He is impossibly handsome in that chthonic way she can't resist. The polar opposite of what lay inside Worth all those years...

"We don't have to talk," she says, half to herself.

"I don't know what to say, Christabel," Kalum explains. He slows the car down and turns onto a back road. Pebbles grind under the tires, crunching as he comes to a stop. "I think I just wish we had met under different circumstances. I've been here with Mother so long I've started to forget that there are other people like us. And once this is over, we'll go back to guarding the pit of Hades, just like always."

Christabel has never entirely understood what it is about her that inspires men to pour out their souls. What she used to find charming she now finds irritating and, truth be told, quite tiresome. But now is not the time for yawning.

"Kalum, I need you to focus on the matter at hand. We don't even know if life will ever get back to normal."

He sighs. "You're right."

"From our conversations, I'm assuming the villa itself is about a half a mile up that hill and toward the seaside," she says, summoning as much sweetness as she can muster.

He looks confused a moment and then nods.

Guilt-stricken, she adds, "We can talk about your family inheritance after this is done, yes? Presuming we're not all sucked into the endless void and suffering for eternity?"

Kalum nods. "I see your point."

"Good," Christabel says. "Now, you've got a job to do."

When they come to a stop at the base of a hill, she doesn't wait for him to open the door for her. Instead, she hops out of the car and stretches in the riding pants she acquired for the trip. It still feels rebellious wearing them, but she started doing so ten years ago, and she isn't about to stop.

"Now, let's go over the plan again," she says, not unkindly.

Kalum grins, a little brightness in his eyes despite the dark. "I wait here until I see you come back or see your friends. And then I give them instructions and tell them what's going on if they don't already know. But...how will they know where to find you?"

"Alma can always find me," says Christabel, tapping her forehead. "And I suspect Kit can, as well. I've got a distinct olfactory imprint."

* * *

It's been some time since Christabel took a physical role in their business, having preferred the academic slant for the last decade or so. She worries at first that she'll be incapable of scaling the side of the hill, but once she gets moving, it's easier to recall her abilities. She had, after all, traveled the Egyptian underworld with Worth, so long ago, before he had transfigured. It had been ages of walking, and at one point she had found herself in full unicorn form.

Christabel takes a break just before rounding the last corner. She can see the back pathway now, to the south side of the villa and barely in view of the sea. Not much further now. She takes a deep breath and closes her eyes, wondering just what it is she's up against. And if she sees Vivienne, then what? Do they talk about Worth? How would she even begin to explain what happened...

"Monoceros."

Of course, he would show up.

Of course.

Turning slowly, she isn't surprised to see him. She didn't heard him approach; she never does. Another Olympian. A *certain* Olympian. He smells of aged wine and olives.

Hermes.

"Why do you all insist on calling me that?" Christabel tries to make light, but it is just in the hope of delaying the inevitable.

"Because it makes your nose crinkle and it's *adorable*."

"Hermes, please."

"Come now, Christabel, have you entirely lost your sense of humor? You were never so frigid with me."

"We are at war. *You're* at war, and you have time for teasing." She is glad of the dim light because her cheeks are on fire.

"Oh, my darling, I have been at war for so long I scarcely know the difference," he says, his voice deep and sad. It makes Christabel want to be in his arms again, to smell his rich scent, and bury her head…

She coughs. "I ah, well, regardless. I need to be on my way, and I don't want any distractions."

"I'm a distraction now, am I? How delightful."

"Hermes. Please."

"Ah, well. If we are all business, I suppose I ought to at least do my duty. I've got a message." He says it proudly, coming more fully into the sparse moonlight. Not that he needs it. Christabel is reasonably certain, and her research supports the hypothesis, that Olympians don't need a light source to be visible. They each have their own inner network of filaments, of sorts, that illuminate or dim their visages at will.

They have met before, and she observed that light very closely. Very, very closely.

Hermes nods, a look of merriment in his eyes. All of him is merriment. Somehow, he is composed of lines of joy, angles of ecstatic motion. He is at once handsome and beautiful, his dark hair falling into his eyes just below a thick band of leather. His body is pleasing, tastefully robed, dark hair on his forearms, chest, legs. And a dark shadow on his strong, fine jaw. She'd kissed it before, and it *was* delightful.

He pauses before speaking, drawing a long breath. "Ah, darling, I forget you are indeed the most beautiful of your kind."

"It's a certainty when I'm the *only* one of my kind," Christabel says, trying to stall while she considers the what the message might be. "Flattery will get you nowhere."

"A god can hope."

"Not if there is no god."

"Yes, Artemis is up there, isn't she? Ah, well, serves her right. I won't be risking my life and limb," Hermes says, sounding almost bored. "I wasn't even planning on coming here, of course, but then Apollo was so up in arms and, well, I can't very well avoid my duty. And he is so insufferably annoying when he's in a snit."

"Apollo sent you?"

Hermes laughs, and it's like a rushing stream. Christabel thinks for a moment that she would like to bathe in that river water, surrounding herself with his undulating laugh, and then she chides herself at the scandalous thought.

"Apollo? No, he doesn't care about you, darling Christabel. No offense."

"None taken."

"It's from the *celestial*. He's with Apollo now."

Damn, then Hermes didn't come of his own volition. It stings a little. She thought she'd gotten over Hermes years ago, after the incident on the Seine, but apparently not. Curse her hot blood and her cold heart.

"I don't...I don't want to read the message."

"No worries, love. No reading necessary. It is merely a message. No print. No scribblings. The good, old-fashioned way."

149

Christabel frowns deep enough that she can feel it twisting toward tears. Not now. Not now. Not now.

"I am trying to save a goddess. I don't have time for Ophaniel."

"You think *I* do? The last thing I wanted was to visit *you* after being so entirely rejected last time."

"Hermes, this is serious."

"It's *always* serious in my family."

She wants to hit him. And kiss him. And it's very confusing. "You don't seem terribly bothered that your cousin, or sister, or whoever she is, might be just moments from destruction."

Hermes scratches the side of his face in a very human gesture, as if his scruff is itching him. Then he shrugs. "I've been around awhile, little *Monoceros*, and while it may surprise you that I'm not rushing to my niece's aide, remember that we're all quite monstrous in our own right. Remember? You fought to prove it. Artemis plays the blushing virgin, whether by necessity or choice, but she's made a lot of enemies. I warned her against this. I even cleaned up after her a few times. I believe you know Vivienne du Lac? That nymph and I have a history. Not like our history, mind you, but, well, if I'm doing this for anyone—as if I had a choice in delivering messages—it would be on account of her. And you, of course."

"So she *is* a nymph," Christabel says, the delight of being correct welling up in her, almost making her laugh.

"Of course, Vivienne du Lac is a nymph. 'Night sylph'? How laughable. I once gave her the chance for another life. Better than going tits up in a fountain like Ovid claimed, don't you think?"

"You mean… *Aura*…"

"You do remember your Ovid."

"My goodness, I presumed she was of god stock, given

her age and her astounding abilities, but I've not had a chance to observe her, and while I had about ten candidates I didn't think that she could be *Aura*, of all people. Gods..." The ramifications of what happened to her...

"As delightful as your epiphany is, I suspect that Cygna and her cronies are attempting to win Aura—Vivienne—to their side because they need her for something. I've no idea if she'll take the bait. And your friends aren't too far away. Apollo is bringing them by chariot, if you'd believe it. It's a rickety old thing, but it gets the job done."

"Chariot? That will take too much time. I can't wait."

Hermes shakes his head, looking over his shoulder. "Ah, darling. Apollo's chariot does not go overland." He squints up at the sky, then nods to himself. "You've got at least an hour. Some of us can flit in and out of space; others cannot, especially with a chariot full of riffraff. The dwarf will arrive shortly, though. I can feel her rumbling."

"Well... thank you. I think. I suppose I should be going now."

"The message?"

"I don't want to hear it. Not if it's from Ophaniel. You know about the two of us, Hermes. There are just some things too painful to face head-on."

"I have to deliver it before I go," he says, and he does sound sad, remorseful. He holds out his hand and touches the side of her arm gently.

"No..."

Christabel starts to run, not certain that she's fleeing from the message or Hermes. As if running would matter! Fear of knowing courses through her body, and for the first time since Worth's transfiguring, she feels her form expanding and filling up new space. Her face elongates, her legs lengthen. She feels her chest swell and her hair

151

streaming down her neck. She is on all fours, but then all fours is all she has.

Still, unicorn or no, she cannot escape the words of the god.

"'When I fall asleep, I still see you smiling behind your coffee at El Fishawy.'"

It was a thousand years ago. No, ten years ago. Yet it was so long ago. Across a table, hands brushing, hot coffee streaming up into her nose. His face. Her eyes. She buried it so deep that it felt like it would fossilize. But those words, those places. Cairo conjures up around her in dazzling beauty, a confluence of sounds and smells and the feeling of promise.

That love was possible.

That maybe…

Christabel collides with a rocky outcropping that appears out of nowhere.

But wait.

"Whoa, whoa, Christabel!"

It's Alma.

* * *

Alma has been waiting because that's what she was told to do. Though, she isn't waiting simply because she was told to do it; she agrees that it's the right call. She can travel distances far faster than those around her, save maybe that celestial, but that doesn't mean she would put herself in danger storming into an unknown situation.

She's dealt with gods before. They were enemies, mostly. Except for Loki. He has always understood her kind better than the rest of the haughty pantheon.

Regardless, she is not dealing with Loki or Freyr or any of

the gods she's met personally. It's been so long that she's felt a proper dwarf, but that's not what's bothering her.

What bothers her is that the earth itself feels wrong here.

Finding her friends was far more difficult than it should have been. Usually, she can sense their individual reverberations above her head as she's traveling through the rock veins. But once she arrived about one hundred miles below this actual location, the signals became very difficult to read.

Thankfully, and for the first time in at least ten years, Christabel shed her human visage and went full unicorn. That is strong enough, at least, to pinpoint where Alma should be. And so, as she feels it happening, half sleeping-below the rock, she shudders as the thermal energy of unicorn power careens down through the Earth, and Alma finally has a guide star.

Coming up through the layers of soil is not an easy task this time, however. The ground itself resists Alma as she presses up and through. Usually, the energy exerted is primarily mental, ensuring that she geolocates correctly. But now the resistance burns her skin and makes her eyes see double.

When she finally emerges, Christabel— more or less in her unicorn form, though she's got some stripes this time and her horn is striated—is barreling toward her at top speed and Alma has to shout to get her attention.

"Christabel!"

Christabel rears back, shaking her silver-grey locks, her oversized dark eyes reflecting like glittering stones. To Alma, in comparison to the rest of her horrid friends, this form of Christabel's is the only one worth writing home about.

But it's still terrifying, too. She isn't big, but Christabel possesses an absurdly heinous amount of power when she's in unicorn form. Alma doesn't think she quite understands that.

"Well, at least I found one of you." Alma crosses her arms and levels the unicorn with an even glance. "I thought you weren't looking like that any longer."

"I... didn't know if I could." Christabel shakes her head as if trying to dispel a fly. "It's off around here. I started running away from Hermes, and I just felt my guard slip."

"Hermes again?"

"I don't want to talk about it."

"Very well, but where are the others? I tried to find them, but it's as if they've lost touch with the earth entirely."

"That's because they have. Hermes told me that Apollo let them use his chariot."

Alma blinks and looks toward the starry sky streaked with fog. "That'll make for an entrance."

"If they get here soon enough. But we must hurry. It's not far from here."

It's a good deal more difficult for Christabel to scale the side of the villa due to her hooves and all the gravel. Alma has to pace herself in order to keep the unicorn from falling to the bottom and having to start the whole climb again.

She still doesn't feel right. If there are more bleaknesses about, perhaps that's the trouble. But it is a great deal of sensation for such little creatures. Well, presuming they're still little. Could they be larger?

For once, Alma wishes she was chattier. But she says nothing as they make the ascent together, just looking over her shoulder now and again to Christabel, who does not meet her eyes.

At last, they reach the side of one of the buildings. It's overgrown with vines, and certainly not naturally. From where Alma sees it, the vines are a latticework of art, a filigree of most delicate craft. They twine up and through one another, a dizzying knotwork that recalls old Celtic jewelry. Yet sharper. Purposeful.

It takes just a moment, but Alma sees a flicker at the top of the vines where there's a small window. From all directions little moths fly around, converging at the pinnacle.

"It's beautiful," Christabel says, finally catching her breath. The moths float about in their own dizzying cadence, back and forth, back and forth, making a wild dance of intertwined movement. "It's...Vivienne!"

A silhouette in the window. The smooth brow, a sharp nose, a neck carved as if with a sculptor's hands. The moths are all trying to get to her, through to her, as are the vines.

But someone is there with her. Someone looming over her. Someone making her scream.

18

A SIMPLE SUPPLICATION

Vivienne didn't give them an answer. How could she? Now she sits by her small, moonlit window, stroking Nadine's warm brown hair, letting the strands slip through her fingers repeatedly. Nadine fell asleep weeping, and Vivienne wishes she had it in her to cry again. She feels sorrow all around her, like wings unfurling behind, wrapping her in a cold, impossible future. Tears do not come, though. Just a simmering rage.

The metal on her wrists prevents her from truly feeling; from touching that power inside herself.

Cygna is not wrong, Vivienne thinks. And that makes her plight all the more complex. The Olympians have always been monsters—but they have also changed. Perhaps not Artemis. But Hermes, certainly. And Hades, who was ever given the wrong side of things, Vivienne felt. To say nothing of Aphrodite. The few times they met, she was kind, gracious, a kindred spirit. She almost felt like family.

And now Vivienne remembers because she must. She remembers everything. She digs through the permafrost of her memory, the one power the shackles cannot contain. It is painful, like breathing fire, but it must be.

Nadine stirs, eyes flickering open, as if sensing the shift in Vivienne. Her brows are like smudges of smoke on her dark face, and Vivienne gives her a reassuring look.

"I'm afraid," Nadine whispers. "I'm afraid of what they'll do. Now I know what they're capable of."

Cygna and Bastille made an offer to Nadine, as well. And revealed the location of Nadine's prime antagonist, a ghoul named Crad. He had been one of the first consumed and put into the void, as they hoped such revenge would endear Nadine to them. But they could not have anticipated the ifrit's fury at having her own revenge stolen.

"They could have just told us to begin with," Vivienne says, the train of thought resting again on the same point.

"Would you have listened?"

"Probably not. I'd forgotten who I was before. They reminded me. And now, well, I cannot exactly go back."

"I wish I had that talent, to forget," Nadine says. "I remember all too well. How did you manage?"

Vivienne closes her eyes and goes back to the day she had told Nerissa the same thing. Hundreds of years ago, when she was leaving another life. She wanted to start anew, with Nerissa.

"I would tell myself a story," Vivienne says. "I would do it every morning and every night. I would tell myself the story of my new life so many times that eventually it would come true."

"What about your old story?"

"I locked her away. I locked away her pain, her grief, her monstrousness. I see now, that she was just caged. We may be horrors that walk the earth, capable of destruction and power, but I know we are only these marvelous beasts forced in cages again and again. It is no surprise we lash out."

"So, who are you now?"

It wasn't a question Vivienne knew how to answer. "I think my methods are fraying, my dear. Now that I see what I've become, who Vivienne is as a slave, I begin to wonder if all the baubles and details I fashioned for myself were nothing but lies. I wanted to be better, to value human life and mortal existence. I wanted to use my powers for the betterment of the world. Now all of that has been taken."

"Mortals deserve what's coming to them," Nadine says softly.

"Perhaps. But I do not think we are to judge. If we rip apart their deities, if we obliterate everything they believe in, where does that leave us? We are less monstrous because we know better, I think. I find some comfort in that. In our capacity to love, to grow, to move through our mistakes and become..."

Vivienne does not finish. The door swings open to reveal Bastille, dressed in a red smoking jacket and preening. Although Vivienne is no longer what she'd consider at the height or center of fashion, she still knows poor style when she saw it. Bastille is a handsome fellow, gifted with all the strengths a masculine form could wish. But he always pushes his sartorial volume just a little too high.

He is obviously proud of himself. He only wears red when he's feeling sure of things.

Bastille doesn't look at Nadine; he's been ignoring her as of late. "Ah, there's our nymph of the hour," he says. "Have you had time to think over our proposition?"

Vivienne feels that ache at the base of her skull, reminding her that her power is dampened, not stopped. It leaves her breathless. Reminding her that she is Aura. That she is rage. That she is a child of Titans.

But she summons up her brightest smile and keeps her teeth to herself. "I still need some time."

It's worse than usual, the dampening. But as one might worry away a thread in a great tapestry with care and precision, Vivienne feels her own memories slipping through the vice of her shackles' power.

She feels her own magic flicker, feels the pull of a familiar soul…if she cannot escape from here, she can at least let herself be known.

But it takes a great deal of energy. Once Nadine sits up, and the heat dissipates from her lap, Vivienne has to force herself to stand. She does not like letting Bastille lord over her.

He smiles, teeth flashing. "There are many things I can give you, darling. I can give you the finest silks; I can arrange for the best music this side of the Atlantic; I can set a meal for you that would make your toes curl just to smell. I can even let you free of those shackles. But I'm afraid time is the only thing we don't have."

Vivienne does not want any of this. She only wishes that she'd had a chance to explain better to Nerissa. Perhaps it is better, for all of them, if she simply rolls over and does what they ask. They need her power, her magic, to strengthen the connection to the Silence, that great center of negative energy in the cosmos from which Cygna draws her power.

"It isn't so simple," Vivienne says, trying to bring a diplomatic tone to her voice, but finding it sounds frail to her ears. "I am all for revenge, you know. Except, in this case, I feel as if I am being threatened rather than asked."

"We couldn't be sure who you were until Cygna returned, and until Artemis confirmed," Bastille said. "It was no easy task bringing her here; it took centuries of planning. You wouldn't understand, I don't think, the sacrifices she had to make in order to evade the eye of the Olympians."

"I don't blame her. Unlike me, no one took pity on her. And those who are bereft of pity often fester," Vivienne says.

"And you defend the Olympians?"

"No, I do not. But nor am I certain that casting them into the Silence, or whatever clever name you've deemed for your doom and gloom, is the best method for revenge. I'm still not even certain how you came by her in the first place."

Bastille grins again, his fangs lengthening. "Oh, well, that's a delightful story I believe you'll find a rather fitting irony. You had a connection to a certain Christabel Crane, did you not?"

It's hard for Vivienne to forget the woman who stole Worth Goodwin's heart for good. But she tries not to let the sound of the name impact her expressions. "I did."

"Well, in the last twenty years she's been quite busy. Publishing material, traveling the world, and most recently, working on a truce between the deities and the monstrosities. The legal proceedings were lengthy and, to most, rather boring. But we found a fascinating pattern among the testimonies, and enough to lead us back to the Olympians. Artemis was just the first. While she was not directly involved in the treaties, Hermes, Hades, and Hestia featured considerably. It did not take long to trace the paths."

It does not sound like Christabel. But then, what does Vivienne know? It has been the longest twenty years of her lifetime, and Christabel is so young.

"I would like a chance to speak to Artemis, tête à tête, as it were. Would that be possible?"

"Alone, no. But I would be happy to accompany you if you believe speaking to that shameful creature would aid you in your decision. Because, and I truly don't mean to drag things out, darling, but we'll be able to channel your powers one way or another, you know. The bleaknesses can take what we ask; we believe that your ultimate cooperation will be less...messy. We did just get the mosaics clean."

* * *

"The vines…" Christabel whispers. The vines are moving up toward Vivienne's window. They can see her speaking to a tall man wearing red, the lamplight limning his dark, oiled hair. Vivienne's voice carries, and Christabel cannot hear the words, exactly, yet she knows…

They spoke her name.

"Shh…" Alma is not in a mood to speak.

"But if Vivienne is truly powerless, how is it that the vines are…"

"Shh!"

Christabel settles down, huffing. She can't very well climb the vines from where she is, but watching Vivienne gives Christabel a sense of calm, even as fear trembles through her.

What would she tell her? How would she tell her? Worth is dead. The man they both loved was never real to begin with. He was a trapped angel, trapped for his protection by a woman who may be some kind of Ur goddess—Christabel is convinced that Dr. Frye is beyond a deity—because an Egyptian goddess wanted him dead for falling in love with a moon god.

The moon, as if in mockery, slips away behind a cloud and Christabel closes her eyes. Her tears sting, and it's harder to control them in this form. It's been so long since she stood on all fours again; her body feels muddled, confused, and the inner workings are catching up with her consciousness.

"It's alabaster," says Alma, and Christabel hastily clears her throat.

"What is alabaster?"

"Underground," says Alma. "Well, gypsum. And selenite. Massive quantities. It's been hewn into the ground of the villa, sprinkled into the soil. Big, heavy crystals. They're… confusing me."

"*Now* you're confused? I crossed that bridge a while ago," Christabel says.

"It's got a strange property, but I can't remember what exactly."

"The Titans used it on their faces in the war against the Olympians, if I recall. Perhaps that has something to do with it."

There is not, however, time to answer, for an immense explosion above their heads and a sound like shattering wood draws their attention upwards.

A chariot is falling from the sky.

* * *

Nerissa doesn't like the idea of flying any more than she likes the idea of driving an automobile, but she steels herself knowing that Apollo's chariot predates even boats, and there is some comfort in that.

The god speaks of his chariot in all manner of glowing terms, and always with a loving, sweet tone to his voice, as one might boast of a favored child. He glides his hands over the golden sides, traces the laurels carved into the ivory, and enumerates a dozen different rules. None of them, however, seem to predicate any safety, for there are no restraints in the chariot, nor are there doors. In the Greek fashion, it is forward-leaning, though certainly large enough for their small cadre, and Nerissa cannot help but notice how perilously easy it would be to fall backward and into oblivion.

There are horses—of course, there are horses—but Apollo glosses over them quickly, returning to the construction of the chariot rather than the living beings attached to and contained within.

Kit keeps close to Nerissa during the proceedings, asking a thousand questions with her eyes, yet speaking little.

"I feel better, I promise," Nerissa says as they take their seats. "I wouldn't be going if I was feeling ill. You don't have to keep after me like a mother hen."

Kit frowns into the scarf she's wearing. "I am not a chicken," the *kitsune* says with a half growl. "I am concerned."

"I know you are. I'm sorry about that."

"Why are you sorry? There is nothing to be sorry about, Nerissa." It's more words than Kit has said in hours. Nerissa is both elated and a bit disappointed; she was enjoying the quiet, but not the lack of communication. She does enjoy it when Kit gets animated.

"You seem upset?" Nerissa doesn't mean to ask the question, but feelings have never been her forté.

Kit crosses her arms and looks away. "I'm not."

"You look like a petulant child."

"I look like a petulant *kitsune*." When Kit looks again at Nerissa, her eyes are flashing, and her teeth are out.

She is magnificent. Nerissa has never told her this directly, of course, but it's true.

Worth is speaking with Apollo in a low voice, and they have not yet taken off, so Nerissa decides it's as good a time as any to try and bring things out in the open, as much as possible.

"That was not fair of me. I'm still recovering. The arms don't hurt, exactly, but it's a dull ache. And I get confused. The new arm isn't a permanent replacement, or at least it won't feel that way until the rest of me is officially gone. I know my true form is wounded, that those two arms are frozen, painful, but…"

Kit looks terrified. "You…oh! I suppose it doesn't matter. When this is over, and when we've finally gotten Vivienne to a safe place and hopefully not plunged the entire planet into permanent darkness, you'll finally be happy."

"Happy? My dear, happy is not a feeling I strive for."

"But losing Vivienne made you sad."

"You never met her, Kit. It's hard to explain. But yes. It has made me very sad."

"You loved her."

"I did."

"You do still?"

Nerissa sighs, looking down at the nails on her good hand. She has not bothered to cast her glamour fully; in fact, she cannot. To preserve Dr. Plover's work, and keep the pain at bay, she must exist in this half stage, preserving power she would otherwise use in disguising herself. Letting the glamour slip helps keep her own power from waning. There are no mortals around, anyway, and she believes, here on this rooftop in Notting Hill, that she would be incapable of a full glamour in her current state of exhaustion.

"I will always love Vivienne, Kit. She was the one who dragged me out of the swamp and showed me that I didn't have to thirst after human blood."

"You haven't had *implet* in days," Kit points out.

Nerissa hasn't even considered that. She frowns, looking over at Kit. "I can't explain that. I am different from when I entered the in-between place. I know things now that I didn't know before. I am not just a simple lamia."

"And I am not a simple *kitsune*."

"I never said you were."

"But you are not happy with me."

"Kit…how could you…"

Her hearts. Oh, they're beating fast now. When did that happen? Well, Nerissa can't pinpoint exactly when she started thinking about the *kitsune* as more than a business companion. She chose to stay, even when Nerissa gave her freedom. And though Kit talks about three thousand percent more than even Vivienne ever did, Nerissa knew they had a natural kind of companionship.

Kit has the most glorious eyes, and Nerissa has rarely seen them this close. In the lines of her round face, they cut a clever, wild arc beneath her sparse brows. They have no discernible iris most times, but when she is very excited, they flash a kind of amber red. A fox's eyes.

Nerissa takes a deep breath. "We are about to take a god's chariot up into the sky and make a daring rescue to attempt to prevent a goddess from being thrown into the abyss. And not because she has that many redeeming qualities, but because people like Christabel have taught me that such sweeping judgements are evil. Life that seeks to cause pain and torment to other life, to rob it of its innocence and wonder, is worth fighting against, tooth and nail."

"I don't see what that—"

"Kit, hush. Listen. What I'm trying to say is that over the many centuries of my long and storied life, I have encountered some truly incredible creatures—gods, monsters, and everything in between. I'm not sure which category I've always fallen into, but I have made a good show of it, anyway. I count myself very lucky to know so many arcane beings all around the world. But then, I met you."

Those fox eyes kindle. Kit looks as if she is ready to bolt and so Nerissa reaches out and takes the *kitsune* by her arms, wrapping her fingers—metal and flesh—around the meat of Kit's shoulders.

"And I've held you back from all that," Kit says in a half-whisper.

"What? No! Kit. There is no one else I'd rather have by my side."

"But what about Vivi—"

Nerissa leans forward and pauses just a breath before her

lips touch Kit's. In the back of her mind, she wonders what a truly baffling couple they would make—a fox and a snake—and yet, as they make contact, it is the sweetest of matches, the most perfect of melodies. Kit does not resist; she presses back until Nerissa feels her own tongue sweep across Kit's canines.

"Oh, god, finally," says Apollo, pushing past the two of them to get at the front of the chariot. "I couldn't bear another moment of that twisting sexual frustration between you two. It was making me nauseated."

Kit is laughing now, and Nerissa is smiling—as close to a laugh as she gets—and then they sit closer together. Nerissa takes Kit's hands in hers and they settle in as the chariot shudders and rises into the sky. And they kiss once more.

19

WHO ARE WE, AGAIN?

This isn't going to end well.

You are such a killjoy.

I'm not speaking narrowly. I mean, I'm quite aware that we can't live out this situation for too much longer. Whatever we are together, which I haven't quite figured out yet, is...unsustainable.

Thank you for the reminder, Ophaniel.

That Apollo fellow is familiar, but I can't think of where we've met.

I don't think our mythologies crossed too often.

Perhaps not.

You were saying something about inevitable doom.

They are following the chariot, the very one steered by the aforementioned Apollo, not just because they have a pair of wings but also because they simply would not fit. Or at least, at the moment Worth is quite certain Kit and Nerissa need time alone considering that kiss.

Worth is feeling sorry for himself, and so Ophaniel is at the helm in terms of steering, at least.

Oh, yes, and they have figured out how to fly again.

Worth isn't particularly sure when that happened, but he suspects it has to do with his time as the primary consciousness in the body. After all, even though his Glatisant self was merely an enchantment, he was far more familiar with flying.

But he thinks there is something else at play, as well.

They are headed toward Christabel. Ophaniel is loath to admit it, but he, like Worth, is rather besotted with the unicorn. Though they'd only crossed paths a handful of times, the angel is most likely along for this ride primarily so he may see her again. She confuses him.

She is so easy to find. Is she like that for everyone?

Worth doesn't need to ask who "she" is.

Christabel is a unicorn. What that means, precisely, no one exactly knows. I was there, in the room, when she transfigured for the first time, and I can honestly say it was one of the most incredible moments in my existence.

So I was there, too.

Technically, I suppose; you were always there, weren't you?

Maybe that's it. Because I can sense her closer with every mile we close in on Andalusia. That's what it's called, correct? Andalusia?

Yes.

They fly on a while longer through the dark, the whispering whoosh of the wings punctuating the quiet. Now and again, when the wind is right, Worth can hear Nerissa and Kit speak in low voices, or Apollo giving a command to the four flying horses at the front of the chariot. They aren't easy to see; you have to look just right to get a handle on their size. It occurs to him that Nerissa and Kit might not even be aware they're there at all.

Helios, I think. He used to be Helios.

Clearly, this is bothering you. But finding the historical and/or mythological analog for Apollo is probably not something we have the time for right now.

I don't like this Cygna person and her cohorts. We're close to her. And Christabel. Not long now.

You are disjointed, even for you.

I'm having a crisis. I'm not supposed to care for mortals or...anyone other than celestials. My lover is gone from the world, and I am...

You're lonely. You can say it.

I think I was hoping that when I was revealed someone would come for me. One of my celestial siblings, or perhaps a seraph. That there would be a welcoming party for me...that someone missed me. But, Worth, I feel entirely disconnected from the family I once had, from the worship I once had.

Ophaniel, as much as I'm glad you're opening up to me—to yourself?—well, at all, I suppose, I don't think this is necessarily the best time.

There is no best time. I'm a shattered creature speaking to myself as I fly over the Atlantic Ocean in search for a—

The lightning strike—if lightning is the right word for it, Worth cannot say — comes out of nothing and hits the chariot directly in front of where Apollo sits. It's not natural lightning, of that much Worth is certain, because it makes Apollo shout and seems to derail the chariot's trajectory.

And light it on fire.

Also, Ophaniel's wings are aflame.

Except Worth is also on fire because they're sharing a body, and the angel conveniently decides that now is a good time for him to take a back seat.

Steering is a whole lot harder than guiding, Worth decides, especially when wreathed in magical flame; burning is not something he's used to. Thankfully, the altitude is enough that with a few sharp movements, Worth is free of the worst of the burning. And it's nothing more than a few blisters here and there; given the quickness of his healing capabilities, it won't last long.

Alas, the same is not true for the chariot. The lightning strike—or whatever it was—sundered the connection between Apollo and his horses. Two of them are nowhere in sight; one is frothing at the mouth with a strange oil-slick fluid that Worth is sure he's the only one capable of seeing, and the other is trying to turn the entire contraption around in the opposite direction.

And Apollo is not helping whatsoever.

"They cannot fly!" Worth shouts at him, indicating Nerissa and Kit. "You're a gods-damned god! Do something!"

Apollo shakes his head as if dispelling a charm. In the dark, his eyes glow a dim gold hue. He is angry. But he also appears confused.

Thankfully, the god eventually gets his wits about him; even more thankfully, Kit and Nerissa are seasoned monsters, capable of incredible feats. Kit's preferred orientation is generally upside-down, and so she takes this to her advantage as the chariot bucks and begins to lose altitude. Her tails spring out from behind her, a fan of fur and movement, and she uses this as a kind of rudder for the chariot, slowing its flipping and twisting, at least momentarily.

Apollo jumps lightly from the front of the chariot onto the back of one of his steeds which, once connecting with him, comes into more vibrant focus. Worth understands why he had cloaked them before. They're positively radiant, the horses, and also some kind of flying hippocampi.

Another lightning strike, however, hits more directly now, and sunders the chariot from Apollo. His horse, spooked and as bright as a lighthouse beam, begins a furious descent into the shadowy mountains below.

"What a useless assemblage of arcane mass!" Nerissa shouts as Apollo's bright streak begins its sharp descent.

"Grab my hand, Nerissa!" Worth shouts toward her, but his voice is swallowed up with all the whooshing air. "We've—oh!"

He sees her. Christabel. She is far below them, but there is no mistaking the illumination; not just Christabel, but Christabel as a unicorn. As the ground rushes up to meet them, Worth manages to get a firm grasp under Nerissa's uninjured arm, and Kit—unusually light for someone of her build and size, no doubt a *kitsune* feature—wraps her arms around Nerissa's middle.

Just in time, too. A third lightning strike destroys the chariot, flecks of the wood and metal ricocheting out in a dozen directions.

Now it is truly just the three of them and the rushing wind.

It's hard enough to fly on his own, and the wings strain against the resistance, but Worth manages to slow their mad descent now that his wings are not on fire. And Kit continues using her tails to steer them and prevent them from losing complete control.

But it is not going end well. And Christabel is glowing more brightly. And down they go…

* * *

Christabel is thinking about how they are going to get Vivienne du Lac out from under the thumb of her captors when a flaming, falling chariot coming toward her and Alma disturbs her concentration. At first, she chalks it up to a strange side effect of her recent transfiguration back into her unicorn form, but as the sky lights up with lightning —there had not been a storm moments ago, but stranger things have happened—she sees the shapes of her friends up there.

Most clearly, she sees Ophaniel. And she doesn't like that her heart skips in her chest; she doesn't like that she part hopes that he dies from the fall, and also that he finds his way to her so she can look into his face for signs of Worth.

But no, that shouldn't be her focus right now. The focus should be on *helping them* and hopefully without drawing too much attention.

"This isn't going to be pretty," Christabel says, trying to better position herself under the falling forms of her friends. "I'm know I have flying capabilities, somewhere, but I haven't been able to figure them out."

"I've got this," Alma says, and she almost sounds bored. She reaches down and puts her white fingers into the dark, loamy earth. Grunting, the dwarf mutters words in a language that makes Christabel's skin prickle.

But then, immediately, the ground is softer underfoot. Squishy, almost.

"Won't last long," Alma says, wiping her brow with a dirt-stained hand. "But judging by my calculations…"

Any mortals hitting the ground with the force of her friends would have perished upon entry. And Ophaniel is still trailing fire. But thankfully, they are not mortals, and between Alma's groundwork and their own cunning, it's mostly a matter of losing their breaths and having to get their feet under them again.

Kit lands perched on top of Nerissa, her dark hair falling across her face. And there is a smile there. And…Nerissa returns it?

"Well, I hadn't expected to run into you like this, my dear," says the angel. And it is not Ophaniel's voice; it is Worth's.

Christabel's reply catches in her throat as the angel approaches, still clapping out smoldering patches of fire on his wings. His face is not the blank slate of Ophaniel's, that unreadable monolith. It's Worth, with lighter hair but the same broad brow, the same curving lips, the same...

She is delighted she is not in her human form right now. Because she's quite certain she would run into Worth's arms and make a fool of herself, and this is neither the time nor place for such foolishness.

Someone is crashing up the path, and inside voices rise. Of course, they heard it.

There isn't time!

It's Kalum, and he's looking from face to face. "They were supposed to meet us by the road," he says.

"Pardon the intrusion," Worth says, hand to his heart. He is unclothed from the waist up. It is very distracting. "But you haven't happened to see the god Apollo, have you? We lost track of him in the fray."

* * *

Vivienne has only time to see her friends for a scant moment before Bastille clasps her around the wrists and draws her closer.

"I see what this is about now," he says, as if he's gotten an answer to a question that's been bothering him for days. "You're drawing it out. Hoping for rescue."

"I didn't call them," Vivienne says. Was there an angel among them? And something with tails? How much had changed since she'd been away? "Please, let me speak to them. I'll send them away."

The words sound brave, she supposes, but they're not what she feels. For the first time, she feels real hope. That thread is almost free as she pushes down through another layer of her memories, of her true self.

"I thought that twenty years would be enough for you to learn," Bastille says.

It doesn't feel right. Her hands don't feel right. Or rather, they feel *right* when they have felt so *wrong* for so long. They feel cold. They feel strong. Not entirely free from their bonds, but still…

Vivienne risks a glance to the side and sees Nadine there, a look of fear mingled with gladness on her face. And a silver key in her hand, glittering in the cold light of the moon.

That clever ifrit.

Bastille does not have time to react. Vivienne pulls back from him so violently that the shackles fall from her, staying in pieces in his hands. That whole time, Nadine had not been asleep. She had been waiting to free her.

Vivienne does not ask, because outside the window, the cacophony rises, but she knows she must do her best to teach Bastille a lesson.

In years past, she'd stolen the power she needed from others, from those who had loved and trusted her. Like Nerissa, she'd learn to feed on energy that wasn't her primary food, but it worked. Here, there is little of that fuel, but there are plenty of other emotions. Betrayal, memory, the pent-up fury of thousands of years wandering in the wilderness, never quite capable of dying but wishing for it all the same.

She does not mean to change what she wears, but Vivienne transforms quite smoothly before the ifrit and the basilisk. Her hair unties itself, falling in a dark line down her back; a rising tide of silk and frost cling to her body, melting away the old rage and bringing to light the pleasing form beneath. Her eyes go bright, her cheeks flush.

She is Vivienne. She is Aura. She is a daughter of Titans. A monster. A lover. A fighter.

Bastille tries to speak, but Vivienne presses cold into his mouth. Pure, beautiful cold. Ice and air and all, the deepest chill of her soul in a precise and shockingly effective weapon. And then he is on the ground, writhing, unable to scream.

The foundations shudder.

"Nadine," says Vivienne, turning to her friend, seeing her as if for the first time, now that magic is no longer siphoned from her. She is so beautiful, the ifrit. Her dark brows smudged like newly made soot, her eyes fathomless and black as night. Her skin is an impossible hue to guess for it is continually dancing with the light of deep flue flames like one might see in refracted water. "How…"

Nadine stands, holding up a small phial, that glittering slender sliver that Vivienne had seen before. "He was mono-loguing," she says softly.

"You brilliant beast," Vivienne whispers.

The ifrit has that look in her eyes; the one Vivienne knows well: awe.

Vivienne shudders, running her fingers down her pale arms. She feels grounded for the first time in two decades, as if the earth beneath her welcomes her rather than wants to cast her away.

And again, her eyes are drawn to Nadine. Nadine as she should be. Nadine of flame and smoke and power.

"Now I truly see you," Vivienne says. "Come to me."

Vivienne goes to Nadine and pulls her to her feet. Before the ifrit can say anything more, Vivienne pulls her body flush with her own and kisses her deeply. Vivienne traces the lines of Nadine's shoulder blades with her narrow fingertips, feels the delicate lapping of the fire on her skin. Kisses her more. Again. Better. With promises of what they will be once they can come together in their full forms.

A crash from outside. A cry.

"Nadine," Vivienne says. "At last. Freedom is nigh."

"Yes, but I'm afraid your friends…and Artemis…"

Nadine's collar is like a blight on her body. Vivienne's

fingers stop there. "I wish we had time," she says, and she does not mean just to remove the collar.

It is a strange feeling, this love. Before gaining her freedom, Vivienne never thought her attachment to Nadine was this deep. But now she realizes that the intensity was dampened, like all her emotions. If she could freeze time, she knows precisely the matter by which she would attend to the ifrit, and what lines of poetry she might recite, and what cut of cloth she would find...

From below, a shuddering sound.

The ground belches a sulfurous stink.

Hungry, but sated for the first time in a thousand years, Vivienne cups Nadine's cheeks in her hand and kisses her lightly on her surprised lips. "There will be time. Providing we manage to thwart the whole world-ending situation, yes? Then no feat of gods or monsters will keep me from you."

20

FOUR HEARTS OR MORE

F alling to the ground was considerably worse than hitting it. Nerissa had never had the occasion to go careening toward earth like some deranged meteorite, and as she falls, it occurs to her that it's a sensation she does not like. It reminds her of rollercoasters—horrid human contraptions she's only seen from distances—and how not once in her life she has wondered what it would feel like to put herself under such a distressful situation.

And it is even worse than she imagined.

Her hearts beat out of sync, and though she knows she is nigh immortal, given the fact of her recent run-ins with the Void, she wonders if it's possible to explode upon impact. Perhaps it's the pressure change that has so discombobulated her.

Truly the only thing keeping Nerissa from screaming like a flayed banshee on the way down is that Kit has managed to keep her arms about the lamia's waist. It is not as distracting as it might be if they had found their way into this arrangement without the death-defying preamble, but it helps

Nerissa to play over that kiss in her mind a few times before striking the ground.

Nerissa ensures, however, that she takes the brunt of the force. She isn't yet familiar enough with the *kitsune* body to know its weaknesses, and she does not want to take any risks.

Anything for another kiss like that.

Kit lands on top of Nerissa with a breathtaking whoosh, her tails still moving around them, soft fur on her face. She smells like fresh rainwater.

Nerissa looks up at Kit, those amber eyes flashing under her curtain of hair.

"Hello," Nerissa says, her voice huskier than usual. Everything aches.

"Nerissa," Kit says, and how had Nerissa never noticed how perfect her name sounds the *kitsune's* mouth? She could listen to it all day.

"Nerissa!"

Stronger this time, and Nerissa realizes she was falling asleep.

Nothing feels quite right.

Except for the pressure of Kit on top of her; that feels very right.

* * *

In one brilliant moment, the vines twining their way up toward Vivienne turn to ice and Christabel comes face to face with Worth Goodwin.

From her vantage point, the effect is mostly a physical one; where she was warm moments before she is now frigid. The little ice crystals made it onto her hair and her eyelashes, and she stands staring down at Worth, trying to blink and rearrange his body so it makes more sense.

But no. It is his face. Plus wings. And an unearthly light that reminds her of her sweetest dreams come to life.

"Christabel."

She is shaking. Shaking! What an embarrassment. A woman of breeding and intellect falling weak at the knees— all four of them at the moment—in the presence of her once paramour.

"Hello, Worth."

Christabel is quite proud of herself. She sounds calm, reserved, unbothered. There is a great deal of chaos happening all around them, including the appearance of someone who most certainly must be of Hades itself, and yet she can do nothing else but look at Worth.

This new Worth.

But his eyes are the same. How many nights did she try and bring him back out of Ophaniel, until the damned angel infuriated her so much? Until he told her that he found her disgusting and disquieting, and she finally had to leave London altogether.

"It took me a while to find my way back to you," Worth says. He takes a step toward her, but his feet don't disturb the ground. "I'm sorry."

"I gave up on you," Christabel says. She had hoped to take a step backward but somehow ended up a little closer to Worth.

"I know," Worth says.

There are so many other things she wants to tell him. About Hermes. About love. About her research. About the works she's done with Dr. Frye. About the fact that no matter what she's done, no matter who she's met, she always comes back to Worth. And losing him the way she did, outside the realm of mortality and immorality, has continually driven her to the brink of despair.

How she hasn't been able to turn herself back into her unicorn form until now.

But he's looking at her, and he sees her. Christabel. Not the many forms she takes or the masks she wears, but her. Entirely. Laid bare. And she sees him, the Worth she loved from the moment they met.

Though, truth be told, the frothy blood that sprays across her face interrupts the romantic atmosphere somewhat.

* * *

The bleaknesses are far more energized this time, breaking through the ground in a dozen places, and spinning around Alma too fast for her to follow. It's night-time, and that means their darkness is significantly more difficult to spot.

Alma starts throwing up cascades of dirt around her, and that works for a short amount of time until it's clear that the bleaknesses are splitting up around the particles, even as fast as Alma is throwing it at them.

She doesn't like this. And why is everything so cold?

A deep buzzing sound draws her attention out toward the road, and she sees the figure of a man approaching. He is walking determinedly, fists balled at his sides, and he's exuding a particular geological scent: sulfur. Deep sulfur. And then another, more vegetal smell. Alma has a hard time detecting such things, but she senses that it's floral.

Green flame surrounds the man's form; that much is clear as he gets closer. And as human men go, he is rather unimpressive, though he wears a rather fetching leather jacket. Alma decides that if she makes it out of this situation all in one piece, she'd like to get herself one. Christabel shouts his name: Kalum. But that isn't his name. He's of the Underworld, and that is a language Alma knows well.

Alma has spent most of her life away from these sorts of people, but she's quite certain she's looking at Hades. Or at least, an extension of him. There is just too much power there.

And she's happy, because the moment Hades—or Kalum —appears, he begins blowing green smoke across what has now become the battlefield. It makes spotting the bleaknesses much easier.

But also much more difficult. Because there are so many more than a dozen of them, and they seem to be growing, coalescing. Too many for this group. She will have to distract them, lead them somewhere with more stone.

* * *

Worth doesn't feel the bleakness crest his shoulder until it's too late. It saws through his flesh hard enough that Ophaniel rises, taking momentary control.

Not these things again. I'm going to get us out of here.

No! Not now!

This is not your body.

It's not entirely yours, either!

I don't have to stay here.

Look at her and tell me you don't love her.

The pain comes again, and it's impossible to make a coherent sentence internally or externally. But with it comes a fury, too, and Worth is glad of it. Of all the emotions he and Ophaniel share, that is one far more familiar to him and one he can more easily wrest control of.

Christabel rears, and she is such a glorious sight. There is a streak of blood—his blood, he now realizes—across her perfectly white muzzle. She begins to emit a bright light, a clear shimmer refracted along her body in a spectrum of color. She stomps her foot three times on the ground and then begins to move forward, slashing the air with her horn.

Worth is initially terrified. He just wants to hold her. But he sees that the bleaknesses do not like her. They shy from her. And on the other side, the new arrival, the one that Christabel called Kalum, is making the little monsters easier to see.

Buffeting his wings as best he can, though he's almost certain he would not manage flight even if he wanted to, he's able to keep redirecting the green smoke from Kalum toward Christabel, and time and again she slashes at the air.

"Be careful!" It's Nerissa, her voice hoarse. She survived the fall, but she does not look well. She looks confused, her face lit by the green light, her hair down around her in a nest. Worth realizes that she's not in her glamoured form and has not been for quite some time. Likely longer than he's ever seen her.

Which is unusual.

And there is Kit. And she is entirely covered in hair, her mouth elongated and her teeth flashing. She is furious, Worth can tell, but he can't quite understand why.

Except, well, now *that* makes sense.

A bleakness appears from the assembled smaller ones, large and ominous, a gaping maw in the center of them all. It absorbs all light and looking at it makes Worth feel dizzy.

Then a woman emerges from it, stretching her arms lightly as if she's just taken a good nap. She wears white leather, and she brings with her a burnt smell, like after a lightning strike. A beautiful woman, to be certain, but cool. Too cool.

"I'm sorry to interrupt this little revolt going on here," says the woman. "But if you don't settle down, I'm afraid I'm going to have to throw your friends in with the others I was planning on destroying tonight. And really, all I was hoping for was a little conversation."

It shouldn't be a threat, and yet it is.

No.

Ophaniel, what is this?

She has seen the blackness of the center of the stars. She has named the unnamed. She has made it hers.

And then Worth can see nothing but the faint glow of Christabel's horn in the distance.

* * *

Vivienne walks over Bastille, floating as she used to, and takes a moment to crunch her icy heel into his pretty face. It won't last, and she hasn't had the courage to kill him, yet. But it feels good.

She takes the ring from his finger, and he whines.

"It protects me…it's holy…"

"Holy? Hardly. It's a fluke of physics. But for now, the bleaknesses will leave Nadine alone." Vivienne gives the ring to Nadine, and the ifrit slips it on. She shudders.

"You should wear it," Nadine says.

"No, you are not yet whole."

Nadine blazes behind her and Vivienne turns, putting her fingers softly on the collar again.

"What else can I do?" Vivienne wants nothing more than to free Nadine, but the collar does not budge.

"Only the hand that placed it can remove it," she says. "And my first owner was not Bastille. Nor Cygna. It was done long ago when another you know was similarly bound."

"Barqan." Vivienne knows without needing to ask, and she closes her eyes against the memory. Once, she was the slaver. Barqan, she thought, was a mere djinni butler, a clever parlor trick for her amusement. But he was never hers; he was Nerissa's. And for all the decades of his imprisonment, he sought to undo her.

She does not like to think that Barqan knew what would befall her. That eventually she would find herself in the hands of Cygna and Bastille.

A thought for another time.

"We've never spoken of my father," Nadine says softly, and Vivienne cannot help but make a sharp gasp.

"I should have suspected. You are of his ilk."

"I should hate you," Nadine says. "I used to hate you. And then…"

"Shh, I know. It is not the time, love."

And saying that word, *love*, fills Vivienne with an ebullient hope, and with that hope a power she has not tasted in two decades. Reaching a hand out to the solid door, she presses the pent up energy into it, and it turns to frost just for a moment before it shatters.

The house is madness, with the attackers at the gate, and while Vivienne and Nadine are no doubt an incongruous sight, they know every turn of the villa in ways the others do not. It is the blessing of a servant, Vivienne realizes suddenly, a gift she had never anticipated needing.

She must quell her frostiness a bit, and it pains her to do so. But her concern is short-lived. A sulfurous mass belches outside, and the very foundations of the villa shake.

"I do believe that Artemis should pay for her crimes," Vivienne adds, almost off-handedly as they make their way toward the basement. "Just not this way. Right now, she is a significant hazard."

Getting to Artemis is not as simple as merely going through a door, regardless of how much frost power is behind it. There are locks. And guards. And mechanisms in place. Vivienne remembers most of them from her time following Bastille around, but she's afraid to encounter something outside her realm of capabilities.

She is cautiously pressing toward one of the doors on the way to the basement, however, when the wall around it begins to crumble. Another quake. This time enough to set her teeth on edge. Where is that coming from? And what on earth is it?

Holding up her hands as debris rains down, Vivienne is able to make a kind of shield for them, pebbles pattering over the solid ice.

Nadine looks up, and Vivienne would normally be glad to see the look of wonder on her face, but in the unfortunate impending doom of the universe, there is little she can do other than make a mental note for the off-chance they escape with their lives.

Without her shackles, Vivienne wonders how she missed Artemis's presence the first time. She couldn't consider her a mother, not in the technical sense, but as Vivienne descends into the villa basement, her senses flood with memories of Aura, of who she was before.

What kind of creature are you?

But then the memory that comes isn't of Aura at all. Or Artemis.

It is Nerissa. Bedraggled and sitting in filth, the remnants of a dozen beasts and men around her like a carnivorous magpie's nest.

Perhaps we met in another life.

Vivienne is blinking back tears, unable to focus for a moment. The room is shaking again, and that is no pleasantness. They reach the lower landing and through the dust and refuse of the basement—lit the old-fashioned way with torches —Vivienne spies the mass of gypsum where Artemis had been.

It's almost covered her entirely. She's impressive, even as

a malformed statue that looks more like a lump of clay than a goddess. One dark eye peers out from glittering scales of alabaster and mica. She wouldn't need to breathe, of course. Gods never do. They are not made of flesh, not in the strictest sense.

But Artemis is afraid.

Too quiet. No guards. It reeks of a trap.

Vivienne has, despite her rather wispy appearance, managed quite well in terms of physical fights in her past, though she gave up fisticuffs a few hundred years ago. It's been a while since she's practiced, and she is keen enough to sense her own power flickering unpredictably. But she's willing to try.

A muffled noise from Artemis, and then the ground opens in an impressive geyser of chalk and dirt, covering almost everything that wasn't already alarmingly dirty in a fine white powder.

Two things emerge from the ground: one is a dwarf woman. She is of the Nith, Vivienne believes, a reclusive ground-dwelling creature from the wild North with no pigment and no manners. She thought they wouldn't deign to spend time around creatures of her ilk, but here she is.

And the dwarf woman is certainly helping Vivienne, as she's attacking the thing that comes behind her with gusto. It's a creature of negativity. A void being. Vivienne had seen smaller ones before, pets that Bastille was training up. This one is much larger. Its borders appear erratic, unstable. But all light and feeling vanish upon contact.

Except the dwarf has a method to the madness. She is casting chunks of stone—which she seemingly lifts from the ground as if they are naught but marshmallows—and throws them toward the void creature. It slows it, though it doesn't stall it enough to neutralize the threat.

"My fire won't work well, but we haven't tried your ice,"

Nadine whispers. She backs up, eyes wild. Vivienne knows the damage those bleaknesses left on Nadine's body—the torture it took to make her speak—and understands why the ifrit wouldn't rush into the fray.

"See to those outside. Then come back to me," Vivienne says.

The ifrit can walk through walls, so this is no difficult task for her. Vivienne watches as Nadine's figure phases away, trails of blue smoke lingering a breath before the first attack takes her off-guard.

The ringing pain in her body awakens her instincts, though, so Vivienne cannot be altogether ungrateful. She fought with Nerissa many times. And in other lifetimes, besides. Many times, she fought demons in her mind; other times, actual demons.

The void creatures are worse, though. They are harnessed neutral chaos. It's only the rings her captors wear that keep them from devouring their masters. Vivienne was never much for magic rings, having thought them fairy tales and dull superstition. But these rings are something else. A kind of fusion between science and the arcane, and they are powerful, indeed.

When the dwarf woman makes eye contact with Vivienne, she nods in return and calls another ice wall, this time up and at an angle that throws the void creature—now heavy with stones—off balance. The abrupt change in temperature does the trick. But it also encourages attention in her direction.

Vivienne closes her eyes a moment, whispering her apologies to Nerissa, to Worth, and to her friends. If it ends here, in the dark basement with a Nith dwarf and the imprisoned goddess of the hunt, then so be it.

21

JOIE DE BATAILLE

What good is this battle joy without Nerissa? Kit struggles to keep a protective stance before the lamia, her own body shocked from the fall and jittering all over. There are also nerves. Because there was kissing. And it was perfect kissing.

But also, everything in the world is about to be swallowed up into absolutely nothing. So regardless of how good the kisses might have been, Kit understands that daydreaming right now is likely not the most effective strategy. Unless she never wants a kiss again.

The trees around them sway together then, a strange dance orchestrated by the darkness of the bleaknesses. It's hot. Then it's cold. Then it feels as if the center of Kit's chest is beckoning her forward into the nothing that reaches up, up and toward the moon. Smaller bleaknesses rise from the ground all around them, continuing to feed the growing monstrosity. Implacable. Immovable.

Through the nothingness Kit sees stars. Not her stars. Just the nothing stars of nothing worlds grown cold on nothing life; a churning center, a roiling miasma of power.

Cygna stands nearby, unaffected. She is laughing with her head tilted back.

The shiny god-man joins them, looking even more ridiculous in gilded armor and a bright scarlet plume on his head. He glows, at least, though even so, the light is not enough.

Another joins him, and Kit doesn't know the name until someone shouts it: Hades. Except he's not Hades, not really. He's got a body on, like a puppet. And on a regular day Kit might have questioned it, but right now she's more focused on Cygna and a glittering quality in the air behind her.

The shiny man-boy god is not a very good warrior. For all the ornate armor, he is clearly out of practice. Perhaps, she thinks, he is better at inspiring fighters than being one? It doesn't matter.

Nerissa is screaming in pain behind her, suddenly. Kit wheels around, ready to protect her.

"My... arms!" Nerissa groans, clasping at the metal arm with her remaining ones.

But there is no assault. Indeed, the gods are circling Cygna, fending off the bleaknesses; but outside their circle it's relatively safe.

"Your arms?" Kit knows it sounds stupid, and that's the last thing she wants to come across as, but it's hard to think with so much movement happening everywhere.

Nerissa's face, shiny in the moonlight, scales glittering, turns toward Nerissa. "It's...in there..." she says, gasping. "They're..."

But the lamia can say no more.

And Kit understands. Oh, how she understands. The arms are not entirely gone. They are somehow suspended, roiling in that void gathering behind Cygna. And Nerissa's brain is receiving signals from them, except they are no longer attached to her. The pain must be beyond bearing, and that speaks volumes for Nerissa. She is a creature accustomed to pain, numbed to it, perhaps, over the years. Kit thinks sometimes she even welcomes the pain.

Ophaniel and Christabel are fighting, back-to-back, against a kind of bleakness beast that looks roughly like a jaguar full of stars. From the looks of things, Kit doesn't think they'll hold on much longer, even with Christabel's better defense.

They're going to die this time.

And Nerissa is going to die in excruciating pain.

"I came to punish one god," Cygna is saying, "and now it looks like I've got three. Really, I didn't think the family bond extended so far. Especially to you, Hades. You typically stay out of this business."

"This is my holy place," Hades says, the body moving but the lips staying still. Kit finds that makes her even more uncomfortable than the thought of Nerissa's disembodied arms. "You threaten my kin; so I threaten you."

Cygna shakes her head, crossing her arms as if schooling a little child. "Oh, Hades. They always get you so wrong. You're such a delicate soul. I'm sorry for bringing you into this, but you see it's all about the topography, the geological makeup. It turns out that the Titans left behind little clues. It's gypsum you don't like. It's gypsum that will rise and take you; then I will break you and cast you away."

A deep, roiling moan comes from the direction of the house. Cygna's face drops a moment before regaining composure.

"On second thought," she says, looking behind her. "I had thought that I would cast you away, but perhaps you'll be less perishable than the vampires. Voidlings—make them your hosts."

Kit stumbles back as she sees a dozen little bleaknesses

break from the enormous void behind Cygna. And straight toward the gods.

* * *

Christabel knows she is a creature of contradictions, but it still surprises her just how much she enjoys the fight. For a relatively small person, and one with a limited arsenal of attacks, it's not usually difficult to get the upper hand. And though her friends Kit and Nerissa are screaming —she will have to do something about that shortly, she knows—she is rather adept at keeping the little void creatures at bay.

They do not like her horn.

And they do not like Worth's voice.

In all honesty, the sounds he's making wouldn't be appealing to almost anyone, but they do have a certain celestial ring to them. If the voidlings sound like a dissonant reverberation, Worth adds a layer of high, never quite resolving chords. He can make more than one note at the same time. He's always had a variety of mouths, all talented in a variety of ways, whether he was a Questing Beast or a cherub. And she's always been glad, and a little sad, about that. She's never quite put them to use...

But it is exhausting.

She and Worth—or Ophaniel...or both—are naturals together. She doesn't have to worry about his form or style when it comes to the fight. His wings buffet the air enough to confuse the voidlings, who don't seem to have a sentience that Christabel can tell. She's good at sussing that sort of thing out. They are, as she expected, a kind of chaotic nothing. But in that chaos, there is a great deal of unpredictability. Fighting something that *thinks* is considerably easier because there are only so many thoughts one can have when engaged in combat.

Nerissa won't stop screaming, and Christabel tries to get a better look at what's happening across the way, through the blue and gold glow of the gods facing down Cygna.

That scream tells Christabel what her eyes could not.

They are losing.

The gods are struggling against the power of the void. And the void is growing.

Cygna is surprisingly calm through all of this. Though she delivers something of a villain's monologue, she isn't frightened in the least. Christabel senses a calm inevitability about her.

"Worth, this isn't going well," Christabel whispers over her shoulder as she dodges yet another onslaught, the voiding just grazing her ear and making the hair singe and sizzle a moment. "Worth...this is a good time..."

"Not Worth."

"Ophaniel."

"Worth is tired."

"Convenient."

"Worth doesn't know how to fight in this body."

"What do you mean, he—"

Christabel feels the change more than she sees anything, mostly because the light coming from Ophaniel is suddenly so bright that she is momentarily blinded. But she remembers. The first time he transfigured it was no small thing. No elegant angel as he usually presents. It was a creature of flame and horror, mouths and feathers and fury. There are no words to truly assemble his appearance.

Ophaniel is mad radiance, distilled arcana from a profound, celestial realm.

And he is furious.

* * *

Artemis cannot speak, and in many ways, this is an improvement on her person. Unbeknownst to most, she is not a shy, demure goddess. She is a well of stories, and often can't tell when to stop telling her story and allow the flow of general conversation. It's for this reason, Vivienne learned millennia ago, that she had such a revolving door of attendants. Not many can manage more than a few decades around her, regardless of the perks.

But looking upon Artemis now, Vivienne is struck by how terrified she appears. That's not an expression she has ever encountered before, not in her long years as the goddess's attendant. That state of fear is not diminished by the alabaster growing steadily over her neck and face. It has already covered her mouth—thank goodness for little favors —and is almost to her nose. But her eyes remain intact.

Alma dispensed with the bleaknesses with methodical ease, but now they are left with a larger problem.

"I can't move the stone," Vivienne says, shaking her hands. They burn from the effort. She had thought enough cold and moisture would impact the growing cocoon of stone, but she was mistaken.

"I can't shake it," says Alma, her low voice tinged with disbelief. "I can't even *feel* it."

Nadine is the one who hasn't tried yet, having re-materialized after getting a good look around the house, but she seems hesitant to do so. She is not necessarily the lesser of the beings—among monsters, such rank would be difficult to determine, not to mention tacky—but she is nowhere near as predictable. Her collar doesn't dampen her skill entirely, but it does strip away her agency. If Bastille were to wake from his bloody mess, or Cygna to think of it, she could call

Nadine to her. And the power that flows from her kind is at its most potent when it is natural, from the self, not directed.

"Let me at least shed a little light," Nadine says softly.

Alma takes up the rear, watching the exit. The high windows flicker with light from outside, and Vivienne tries to focus on the task at hand.

Nadine walks up to the goddess and puts one hand, limned in blue flame, upon the alabaster. She immediately sucks in her breath as if wounded but presses on.

"Nadine..." Vivienne tries.

"Shh...please, let me concentrate," Nadine says.

Vivienne waits what feels like a half of eternity, tracking the ragged edges as they continue up Artemis's face, the sounds of the battle rising outside.

Finally, shivering, Nadine slips her hand from the alabaster cocoon, nearly falling over. Vivienne is there to catch her, smoothing the hair at the ifrit's brow, feeling her heart ache with the shared pain.

"It's infused with the void," Nadine whispers. "On a molecular level."

"I couldn't see that," Alma says, and Vivienne detects a note of offense in her voice.

Nadine explains. "It's energy. My energy. For what is flame other than that? I can press into spaces with it, explore around. You wouldn't be able to detect the voids because they are...hiding, I suppose, is the right word, in the very structure of the alabaster." She shudders and then seems to regain a bit of strength, her flame rekindling. "It's a cross. Or at least, a structure much like one. And imagine the little spaces between each corner..."

Vivienne gazes at Artemis. The goddess's eyes are full of tears.

"I bet you feel quite terrible now, don't you, Artemis?" Vivienne says, addressing the goddess for the first time. The words almost catch in her throat. "If the world were truly fair, I would be with Cygna in this matter, and I would leave you to a fate of doom. But as it is, I don't think you're going anywhere. The void may be pressing in around you, but Cygna is out there. And that is where I must go."

"Vivienne, that thing is out there," says Nadine.

"Yes, and its primary focus is Artemis, is it not?"

Nadine nods slowly.

"I think I know how to distract it. Nadine, I need you to stay here. Rest. I'd say to make sure that Artemis isn't going anywhere, but I don't think that's going to be a problem."

Nadine almost looks relieved.

"But I'm going to need you with me, dwarf," Vivienne says to the dwarf.

"Alma," the dwarf says. "If you don't mind."

"Very well, Alma. Show me where my friends are," Vivienne says. "I will have to put on something more appropriate, though."

She glares at Artemis before exiting through the cellar steps. "And don't think that you'll simply get away once we free you. *If* we free you. There will be conversations."

As she departs, Vivienne is pleased to see the recognition and horror in Artemis's face.

* * *

Nerissa's life is a long line of pain. She cannot pinpoint exactly when she started feeling this way, but now it is the only thing she is capable of feeling—endless pain, colder than the harshest London wind, deeper than her self-revulsion.

She knows that Dr. Plover isn't really there with her, and yet she finds herself, between moments of absolute madness, having a conversation with him.

"You know, I loved Vivienne for so long that I forgot how to love anything else. And you know, she didn't love me. Not like I loved her. I don't even think she liked me, most of the time. She pitied me, for certain. She wanted to protect me. She feared for me..."

In the in-between world of the void and her dwindling life, Dr. Plover is the size of an elephant. It would bother Nerissa if she thought the bird was real. But clearly, she's in that strange place again, though this time the pain is more insistent.

"You know I haven't had any *implet* in quite some time. Perhaps that's why the pain's so bad."

"No, that can't be it. I honestly don't know what I should be eating, though. I'm not even sure I'm a lamia, through and through."

"Yes, that's a fascinating thought. But I simply don't have enough time."

Then cold. Real cold. Cold on her skin. Her entire body douses in a chill, a familiar, beautiful chill that smells of sea salt and the wandering past. Her world flips upside down, and Nerissa has the strange sensation she's being pulled inside-out, like a sock puppet. So, when she finds herself looking up into a flickering night, the sound of fighting loud in her ears, and the face of Vivienne du Lac looking into her eyes, she does the only sensible thing she can manage: she vomits profusely.

When she rights herself again—taking Vivienne's hand to stand, not because the circumstance makes any sense whatsoever, but because it seems as though it's the right thing to do in the given moment—the wood by the villa is on fire. And imploding. And the villa now boasts a most impressive hole the size of a London omnibus. It looks like a giant doll-house, Nerissa thinks groggily, through spikes of pain and the occasional rational thought. And she can see Artemis, she presumes, encased on the other side of what must have once been a formidable jail cell, glittering in gypsum.

Apollo sees it, too, and Nerissa imagines that this progress must be relatively new for such a raw, roiling sound to issue forth from the god. He starts to rush toward Artemis, but the Hades man—who bodily cannot be Hades, yet somehow must be Hades—prevents him from doing so.

Christabel and Ophaniel—it must be the angel because Nerissa could never attribute such deft, furious, beautiful fighting form to Worth Goodwin—are keeping Cygna occupied. But they are losing. Christabel has dozens of cuts on her white coat, seeping and staining down her sides like a haphazard zebra. And she is tiring.

Nerissa is about to shout out when she feels Vivienne's hand grip her shoulder. She turns to her friend and looks her full in the face. Twenty years she's been waiting to speak to her again, to apologize and to beg forgiveness for a thousand things. To promise her undying friendship. To thank her for all she had done.

But they do not need words, it turns out. Vivienne holds a finger to her lips, little flakes of snow glittering about her like an aura.

Kit is there, breathing hard, a cold mist meeting the air near Vivienne.

Nerissa nods.

Vivienne is stronger than she has ever been, Nerissa is sure of it. Her hair is white, crystalline, her fingernails like talons. Her eyes are pupil-less, just endless pools of water. Where her feet meet the ground, little flowers of frost rise around her, leaving a trail like lace in her wake. She holds on to Nerissa's hand a moment longer before squaring herself before Cygna.

It doesn't take long to reach the immortal human. Cygna is wild with knowing, the void creatures around her obeying her every beck and call. They swarm like mad round birds, relentless and untiring.

"Cygna, Cygna, Cygna…" Vivienne's voice comes from the air itself. No echo, yet strangely resonant. Resonant in every drop of moisture.

"Oh, well, there you go with your dramatics," says Cygna, holding up her hands. "I was hoping for a challenge."

The massive bleaknesses and the smaller ones all halt at once. The living world seems to take in a collective breath. The night lingers on, afraid.

Beside her, Kit is growling. Nerissa tries to reach out with her good hand but instead finds the stumps where her arms used to be. They are knit together with ice. Vivienne…

"What can I say? I've always liked to make an entrance," Vivienne says coolly.

The bleaknesses do not move toward her yet.

"Oh, Aura. Aura, Aura." Cygna says the name, that other name, in a mocking tone. "I was hoping not to have to swallow you up. I really did think you'd make a lovely conqueror by my side."

"I know you've been hurt. You've been broken," says Vivienne, and Nerissa is surprised to hear a note of pain in her voice. Being genuine has never been the sylph's strong point. But perhaps Vivienne is no longer just a sylph.

What you think, you become, Nerissa dear. If you spend all your time thinking yourself a monster, why, that's what you'll be. But in my long life, I've reinvented myself a thousand times. There is great power in the mind.

A thousand times.

For what are monsters, truly? They are not, Nerissa thinks, merely born out of a broken world. No, they are made in the same way of angels and gods. Necessity forms them. It is only their power and visages that terrify those unable to reconcile or be made comfortable around them.

Vivienne looks at Kit. She is so beautiful, so fierce. In the silvery light of Vivienne's power, the *kitsune* is a painfully perfect monster.

"I have not been broken," says Cygna. "I have been *forged.*"

Cygna holds up her hand, ready to strike.

"Fox woman, *now!*"

It is Vivienne who says the words, and they are so counter to what Nerissa is expecting to hear that she doesn't have time to prevent Kit from running headfirst toward Cygna.

22

PRECIOUS

Until Vivienne arrived on the scene, literally forming out of a mist behind her, Kit had been prepared to kill Nerissa herself. Not out of any sense of hatred, but out of love. She could not allow Nerissa to endure any more pain. And even if she could, they were losing the fight. There was no chance they would win; for what is magic good for against the void?

But then, there was Vivienne. Kit didn't need to ask the nymph's name. Perhaps she was a daughter of Benzaiten; maybe she was a goddess in her own land. But it is clear to Kit that, watching Vivienne emerge from a mist before her, that she is more powerful and grand than Nerissa even knew. And Nerissa loved Vivienne. So much so that Kit knows without a doubt whom she is seeing

"Hello, Vivienne," says Kit. She has lost a good deal of her blood and energy, but she is preparing herself for a final fight. And there are tears all over her face. She would have preferred a better introduction. And she would have had more to say. But for once, Kit finds that she has nothing more. The energy required to make words is beyond her.

Vivienne's face is like a carved statue, the lines and curves so precisely made they are at once beautiful and terrifying. She is not very big, and yet her presence extends meters beyond her in every direction. And it is snowing, too. Kit feels the flakes on her lashes.

Kit looks up. The flakes are moving slowly. Too slowly. And beyond them, the other players in the battle are doing the same. Christabel's horn is a blur, arcing as she rears back; Ophaniel's wings unfurl one feather at a time. All but the bleaknesses are slowed to a fraction of their typical speeds. Hades and Apollo are pushed down to the ground, screaming in pain.

"I only have a moment," Vivienne says, reaching out to touch's Kit's cheek. The *kitsune* feels her tears freeze before evaporating. "But you need to listen very carefully. I cannot hold this for long."

Kit nods.

"I cannot do this alone. First, I will take away Nerissa's pain. Then, I will help to trap Cygna in her own game. Can you help me?"

"Yes, I am always prepared," says Kit.

"Good," Vivienne says, her lips spreading in a smile so beautiful that Kit's heart knows why Nerissa fell so deep in love for so long. "I'm going to need your teeth."

* * *

This is the scene before you.

A woman, arms raised, her eyes filled with emptiness, raising her voice in victory. Time hitched, just a moment before, but she was unaware. She is too entrenched in the goings-on about her to notice such a small thing. And there are so many little voidlings to command; so many that she has not quite realized that she is losing control over them. Bastille is no help and might be dead. Her groundlings ran away when the angel arrived, to say nothing of the unicorn.

But Cygna is a woman driven by a desire for vengeance. And yes, she is most assuredly justified in her fury. She, like Aura and Melinoe, our Vivienne and Nerissa, did nothing other than attempt to write lines in her own story.

Is she evil? She certainly looks it. Even her veins are pulsing. She has waited thousands of years as an immortal soul in a mortal body. Unlike Aura and Melinoe, she has never had power, per se. Her metamorphosis was one solely of her own energy. She tried to kill herself, dozens of times, but eventually realized it was of no use.

So, you can perhaps excuse her if, in this moment of near triumph, hoped for in the dark for so many long seasons, she overlooks one of the monsters. It's easy to do so.

For Cygna is looking directly at Vivienne, the one she knew as Aura, and she is outraged and dead set on punishing her. And, to Cygna's eyes at least, Vivienne is the most whole and, therefore, the greatest threat to her. But also full of promise. If Cygna could tap into that power, siphon it for herself…

Cygna does not see the fox woman slink up behind Vivienne, paws frosting in the lacy trail behind her. Cygna does not hear the *kitsune* scurry to the edges, darting around the voidlings.

Vivienne's voice is as cold as the frost of midwinter, merciless. It doesn't matter the words she says; you likely know the sort of thing she is saying. She is a hero, after all. But Vivienne, for once in her life, is not seeking attention for power. She is seeking attention as a *distraction*, and that makes all the difference. For if Cygna truly knew Vivienne in any way, this alone would be enough of a tell. She has made the mistake of thinking that Vivienne is still Aura, but that name and that life died thousands of years before. For Cygna, even her new name did not change her heart.

Nerissa realizes too late that Vivienne is going into the fray.

Ophaniel falls to his side, exhausted, eyes dimming.

Christabel's form flickers back to that of a diminutive woman, her long hair pale down her back covering most of her nakedness. Her tears fall to Ophaniel's wings, but he stirs not.

Hades rages in a green light of fury; Apollo falls when he reaches the border of what used to the villa's wall, seeing his trapped sister.

But Kit goes forward as if she moves in another time altogether.

The frost emanating from Vivienne is about to cross into the negative sphere around Cygna when Kit launches herself. Her tails propel her at an unusual angle, unexpected and impossible to block.

Kit's teeth slice cleanly through Cygna's hand, ripping it off in a smooth motion. She takes one look back over her shoulder and sees Nerissa, arm reaching out helplessly, before she hops into the circle of the abyss.

"Get her! Get her!" Cygna is screaming, but she hasn't realized that the voidlings aren't interested in her any longer.

The ring is not here.

The ring is their commander.

The ring is a circle of bone from a Titan's tooth.

A giant cracking sound shocks everyone to their feet as Artemis finally bursts from the gypsum prison, the minuscule void infusion following the ring to the depths.

The great void grows and grows, calling all the little voidlings home, even the microscopic ones woven into the gypsum. Vivienne helps it along with great sheets of frost and ice, and soon Alma, the dwarf, is doing the same, casting frozen stones into its gaping maw.

The *kitsune* jumps into the void.

"Kit!"

Nerissa tries to scream the name, but there is nothing left of her voice. She has shrieked herself mute.

"Shh," someone is saying, holding her up—all fire and fury.

Then another being comes by her, dark and blurred and familiar. Nerissa feels hot tears on her face, scrambling forward on her knees.

"You must let her go. You must let this be."

She breaks from the hands holding her back—Hades, it was *Hades*—and closes her eyes and searches, searches. The land is ice and fire all around her, and Nerissa is certain that this life is not worth the effort if Kit is not in it. How cruel to have found something so rare, so beautiful, only to see it...

"Do not despair," Hades whispers. "Think!"

Nerissa remembers that voice. From *before*. Before the time she went mad, when she was someone else altogether. Except before she did not think. She despaired, and that despair turned to madness; if Vivienne had never found her...

* * *

Kit feels the stifling end around her. She no longer breathes. She does not need to. She no longer sees, and she is glad of it. She spat out the finger and the ring as she entered, but her momentum was such that she could not stop herself from going *through*, not with all the chaos about her.

There is no time here.

Only thought.

Only madness.

She sings a low song she remembers from before she was herself. She hums the words softly. Or does she? It does not matter. What is Kit is quickly dissipating. She will be in this ever-nothing for eternity. She will not die. She will not dwindle. She will wait, aware...always...

If she had tears to cry, she would fill up the void with them. But she has left Nerissa alive. And the world itself...

But there is yet a little light.

Kit tries to move in the strange space, that which has no laws when it comes to physical movement. She sees a dim light, dwindling, but not far. It shouldn't be difficult to make her way there—

Smack!

A hand slaps her across the face, nails rending at her skin. It's a cold, dead hand, but when Kit puts out her fingers to touch it, she understands. She knows. There, there is the other arm, fingers encircling the other's wrist like bracelet.

And the hands know her, too.

* * *

"Pull her to you," Hades says.

"Bring me closer, grandfather," Nerissa says to Hades.

The god nods. In the distance, Artemis cradles her brother like a baby. She is three times his size, and her tears bathe his small head. He keeps asking her not to fuss, but fuss she does, holding him to her breast and sobbing.

Vivienne restrains Cygna, lashing her to the ground with ice. Vivienne needs only hold up a single hand to keep the spell intact, and Cygna bangs against the walls of her icy prison to no avail. Until the void closes, none of them are safe.

"There we go," Hades says, putting Nerissa gently down before the slowly closing void. It smells like burning, like the ever-present asphodel of the Underworld, but singed.

Nerissa reaches. She closes her eyes and reaches. Not with her good arm. But with the other ones.

* * *

Christabel cradles Ophaniel on her lap and watches, overcome with wonder and sadness. Her angel is cut from shoulder to navel, a great gash that will not bind no matter how many tears she applies. The void has sundered him, and he will not open his eyes. She has already wept for Worth. But now she cries for him again, and for Ophaniel, and for every unuttered word.

"I used to think that my love for you was a kind of curse, you know," she says softly, moving the golden curls from Ophaniel's pale face. His chest rises and falls. Slower and slower. "But now I realize that perhaps it was not a curse at all, that it was a blessing. For who would Christabel be without a heart? Just a blind monster, raging in the dark…"

* * *

The void is all but a sliver, wind still whipping from every angle, when Vivienne finally sees a hint of the *kitsune*. It was a gamble. All of this was. But when the weight of the world and the very concept of existence hang in the balance, one must make some sacrifices.

She just hoped that it wouldn't be so final.

And then…yes. There she is! It is barely perceptible at first, but the void shudders for a moment, and just as it quickens its pace, a clawed hand appears. Then a face, smeared with blood. It is like watching the birth of a great god, Vivienne thinks, and the symbolism is not lost on her.

Nerissa screams, blood-curdling and fearsome, and then Kit is out, pulled by a pair of disembodied arms that, as soon as they appear on the right side of the void, fall limp to the ground, dead.

The lamia rushes forward to the *kitsune*, draping her body over Kit's protectively.

And it is over.

Inasmuch as these sorts of stories are ever over.

The righteous triumph; the wretched fall.

Just in time for tea.

23

OUT OF THE VOID, LIFE

Morgan watches Christabel from across the fire, gauging the young unicorn. She has not been the same since returning from Andalusia, but the old dragon has lived long enough that she's come to expect such changes. All these stories of metamorphoses leave out the fact that we are continually changing, and this is especially true for monsters.

Her story is a good one, of course. Christabel always tells good stories.

"And what happened to them all?" Morgan asks. She knows some of it from Christabel's letters, but due to the sensitive nature of what happened—including the eventual involvement of local communities as well as the Circle of Iapetus—some details were left out.

Christabel leans forward, her eyes glistening in the firelight. Morgan thinks, not for the first time, that Christabel is not a creature of flame or ice, but somewhere in between. A balance. And that must be difficult. For maintaining equilibrium all the time...well, the thought of it makes her uncomfortable.

"Nerissa and Kit returned to London for a time. Dr. Plover was able to form new limbs for her, though I doubt she will ever fully recover," Christabel says softly. "The last I heard they decided to take a tour of Indochine. Then perhaps, to Japan. I warned them that the situation was difficult there, politically, but they are both ever stubborn. But they have each other."

"Well, time will tell," Morgan says. "I'm sure their services will be most appreciated." She pours another cup of tea from the service, adding three cubes of sugar for Christabel.

"I suppose it will. And I suppose we will be around to see it," says Christabel softly. "Not all of us, though. Vivienne and Nadine were last in France. I believe they are opening a kind of parlor there, you know, a salon. So like-minded monsters can find one another. We located Micheaux and his coven; he was frightened, but unharmed by Cygna. Ah, and Cygna. Her trial is due in two months, just after Artemis's. And they will all meet me there. In Prague."

"Prague. What a lovely city."

"Indeed," Christabel says, but there is no joy in her voice.

"Dare I ask about your friend the angel…"

"He did not die," Christabel says. "At least, I don't think so. He diminished. I did not find evidence of his death."

"Well, at least there is that. I don't think it would have been bearable to see an angel die."

"Bearable, yes, where I once imagined I could not withstand such a thing. I have learned that there is much beyond my capabilities. But, Dr. Frye, I am so very tired."

"You are in Scotland. It is a full moon. There is good whisky and a fair wind. My dear, you are due a rest. Why don't you stay here instead of going to Prague? Surely they can do the hearing without you."

But Morgan knows there is no telling Christabel anything. She has made up her mind.

* * *

When Christabel takes the short path back to her cottage, the wind is indeed coming from the west. It smells of loam and good earth and the salty sea, and though it lifts her spirits momentarily it is not enough to last the short walk.

Ophaniel vanished that night of the battle. He asked her to help him up the hill; not with words, but with hand motions and guttural sounds. It was a long struggle up that half-demolished landscape, but they made the ascent at last and stood in the starlight.

She reached over to touch him, but he was gone. Perhaps angels did not die the same way as other monsters…

Happy endings are for the weak, she decides, though she believes quite the opposite if she really thinks about it. It is difficult not to feel sorry for herself after everything. It is not that she thinks she deserves the happiness, but she hoped that love would be enough.

Perhaps not. Perhaps love is the mortar that keeps the wall together, and one must reinforce it with justice, with righteousness, with truth. It is not the love that is the wall; it is the vast sum of it all.

Christabel is just about to turn the latch on her door when she hears a soft, familiar sound. Her heart leaps into her chest, and she does not need to ask who it is when she turns slowly to see him.

Ophaniel. Worth. This being she has loved above all else.

"Hello, Christabel," says Ophaniel.

The angel is smaller than he was before, it seems to her. Somehow diminished. There is a great scar down the side of his body, across his chest and down almost to his navel. And, beside that, speckles over his skin almost like the spots on a cat. Burn marks, she knows, from the voidlings. A deadly reminder of what almost happened.

"Hello, Ophaniel."

"I've come to say goodbye," the angel says.

"I know," she replies. His face, ever still and difficult to read, said nothing of love.

"And to thank you. Your tears kept me from death, from true death. I found my LORD, you know, and he healed me and sent me back."

"But you must go now," Christabel says.

Ophaniel takes a step closer to her and holds out a hand, so delicate and finely wrought.

Her hand slides over his gently, cautiously.

"I must," Ophaniel says. "For a while. I don't know how long. I need to rest. My body is twisted inside out after casting out the darkness, and I need to sleep a long while."

"I'll miss you," Christabel says.

"I know."

"I would tell you to write, but I know it's not your fashion."

"It is not."

"I will think of you often."

Ophaniel kisses her before there is time to wonder at it; before Christabel can say if she had been thinking about it at all. But when their lips meet, she is certain this kiss has been waiting for her all her life. It is so full of love, of understanding, of an unearthly knowledge, that her entire spirit soars.

I have loved an angel, she thinks. *And that is enough.*

The kiss fades, and Christabel sees, through the closed lids of her eyes, the radiance disappear.

Ophaniel is gone.

She is afraid to open her eyes again, to see that blank space. Her hands are balled into fists, and she takes a half step back, steeling herself.

But then there is a hand, warm and welcome, wrapping around one of her own, gently teasing the fingers open.

"I am still here," Worth says. "If you'll have me."

Christabel gasps and opens her eyes. It is no mirage. It is no dream. It is Worth Goodwin, as foppish and darling as he ever was.

"Worth!"

"Perhaps, if you have loved the angel, you can love the man, as well?"

She looks at him, drawing his fingers to her lips, kissing them. He does feel… different. "You're not…"

"A monster. No, I'm not at present."

"But how?"

Worth sighs, shaking his head. "It's a kind of truce. Ophaniel will take a long time to heal. But he is weary. And we both agreed that…well, living as two beings isn't necessarily a bad thing. You are a unicorn. I am a facet of an angel. We both agree that we love you. And so, on the full moon, I am Ophaniel. But the rest of the time, I will be yours. If you will have me."

"As Worth."

"More or less. Certainly, this form only. But who knows? We shall see, shan't we? I can't imagine that Waldemar, Goodwin, and Crane can lie dormant forever."

"Of course not," Christabel says, with a laugh. She takes a step closer and puts her hand on Worth's cheek. It is so warm; so flushed. "We have many questions, and many answers, and many dark roads ahead."

Worth leans forward and wraps his arms firmly around her, letting Christabel sink into him. "I will be here. I promise. As long as you provide newspapers and tea, of course. I cannot live on affection alone."

"Of course, darling. Of course. I shall make you a house of newspapers and tea."

* * *

Dear Vivienne,

Thank you so very much for the lovely hat and trinkets. Kit is quite enamored of the belt; she says the print is from one of the nearby towns where she lived in Japan. How ever did you know? No, don't answer that. I am quite glad that you are using your newfound power for artistic purposes rather than freezing time and crazed monsters.

We have delayed our trip to Cambodia and instead are visiting Bali for a little while. It is a beautiful place, you know, full of the resplendence of the tropics.

No, I no longer need implet. *I no longer need blood. I just need food. Not much of it, but now and again I like a good rare steak if I can get it. Dr. Plover has given me plenty in the way of supplements, mostly copper-based, providing all the nutrients I need without resorting to the darker pathways.*

For all that Bali is lovely, we have heard of a mountain dragon that is currently dining on villagers twice a year. While I do not consider twice a year to be egregious, Kit is insistent that we take a look. So, we shall do.

I have promised to return to Prague, that great city of my heart, in July, and so we will. The tropics aren't exactly delightful during summer, of course, but it's also simply the right thing to do to support our Ms. Crane. Did you hear about Worth? Strangest thing, isn't it? The girl deserves a little brightness, don't you think?

I also plan to visit cousin Kalum and Makaria, as well as grandfather, before I get back to Prague. I don't relish the idea of being back in Andalusia, but those two need company. And it's good to know that I have family...I hope you are reconnecting with yours, if you wish.

Alma tells me of some strange business involving Loki up north. I do not think we have heard the last of Barqan. And Kit wonders if Cygna was, perhaps, just a diversion...

It seems our adventures continue on.

Oh, Vivienne. What adventures we have had. I keep the sight of you, bright and encrusted with frost, holding back the void, every day. And I know that we are as we ought to be. I love you, and I will always love you, but now that I have found Kit...well, you know. I think we were always searching. You will forever be my sister. And I suppose, in some ways, we truly are sisters. Cygna was our sister, too. But we must all hold ourselves accountable. I will look forward to seeing Artemis on the stand, as well, though her trial will be considerably more challenging due to the intervention of Olympus. Who knew they had their own barristers?

Be well, my dear. Say hello to Nadine for me.

I look forward to seeing you in Prague.

Your Nerissa

FIN

ACKNOWLEDGMENTS

In particular, for this book (and this series as a whole), I would like to thank the magical women in my life. I am a skeptic by nature, but having these remarkable humans around me makes me believe in destiny, fate, and the power of divine friendship.

To Olga Alfonsova and Roshi Khalilian and eternal Zug sky theatre, Hamilton singalongs, and raclette; to Kayt Leonard and getting lost in Vienna, almost; to Susan Griffith for twin souls and palates; to Jennifer Hansen, my harmonizing Scandinavian sister who knows my heart; to Carrie and Audrey, who made me an eccentric aunt; and to Jackie Reeve, Andrea Stolz, Marziah Karch, Fran Wilde, Melissa Wiley, and Ruth Suehle, my glittering gals.

ABOUT THE AUTHOR

Natania Barron has been traveling to other worlds from a very young age, and will be forever indebted to Lucy Pevensie and Meg Murry for inspiring her to go on her own adventures. She currently resides in North Carolina with her family, and is, at heart, a hobbit--albeit it one with a Tookish streak a mile wide.

ALSO BY NATANIA BARRON

FALSTAFF BOOKS

**Want to know what's new
And coming soon from
Falstaff Books?**

Try This Free Ebook Sampler

https://www.instafreebie.com/free/bsZnl

**Follow the link.
Download the file.
Transfer to your e-reader, phone, tablet, watch, computer,
whatever.
Enjoy.**

Made in United States
North Haven, CT
03 March 2022

16735495R00138